THE BLACKSMITH'S WOMAN

HER STERN HUSBAND BOOK TWO

R. R. VANE

Published by Blushing Books
An Imprint of
ABCD Graphics and Design, Inc.
A Virginia Corporation
977 Seminole Trail #233
Charlottesville, VA 22901

RR Vane
The Blacksmith's Woman

eBook ISBN: 978-1-63954-018-1
Print ISBN: 978-1-63954-019-8
v1

Cover Art by ABCD Graphics & Design

CHAPTER 1

ENGLAND 1171

The people in the crowded square were all abuzz with merriment, as they were watching the two jugglers perform their tricks. To Beth's ears, the laughter didn't sound joyous. There was sadness in her heart – deep grief she could not push away. Her mother was gone, after a long, arduous struggle with her illness, and Beth couldn't find the money to give her a proper burial. There was nothing left – nothing more to sell, not even a copper coin of their savings which could be used. And Beth knew only too well, no one would hire her now for the hard, honest work she was prepared to do.

Heaving a sigh, Beth found herself nearly pushed against the tall, broad-shouldered man who was standing in front of her watching the entertainment. She managed to keep steady on her feet, and prevented herself from falling against the stranger whose tall form was now obscuring her view of what was going on. It was of no matter. Beth didn't know why she had even stopped to glance upon the jugglers, because it was the last thing on her mind. Her thoughts were in turmoil, and she was thinking only of how to get the coin to give her mother a proper burial.

She smiled bitterly to herself. In truth, there was an easy way to get the money. The lord knight who coveted her body had already offered it to her. She could get coin if she sold herself. And it seemed selling herself was the only thing left to her. Still, it simply hurt to think of it. Beth's eyes were unwittingly caught by the purse which hung upon the belt of the stranger in front of her. She found herself fiercely envying him. A tall, strong man, who was a master craftsman by his garb, and who seemed unconcerned to wear a purse of coin in a crowded square where thieves could lurk at all times. It was plain to her that this man didn't value his coin. By the way he carried the purse, it seemed he truly had coin to spare. His garb was not rich or fancy, yet the cut and the cloth of it were fine. A prosperous craftsman. Just as her father had been before sickness and sadness had fallen upon her home.

Beth was suddenly jostled against the man she'd been wondering about. And somehow, her hand came within reach of his full purse. Coin. To bury her mother without having to sell herself. What if… Beth hadn't ever thought of stealing. Yet at this bleak moment, it seemed the stranger's purse was the very answer to her prayers.

It was as in a dream that Beth heard a shrill voice from behind her.

"Master, watch out! The thief!"

Thief? It was still in a strange sort of dream that Beth understood her hand had somehow already unwittingly clenched around the stranger's purse. And the people who were standing by had already perceived what she'd done in her moment of sheer blind madness.

The moment of weakness had been brief, and Beth swiftly understood she wouldn't have brought herself to ever steal from anyone. Yet it was all it took to seal her doom. The stranger turned to stare at her, grabbing her by the arm, and, to Beth, his dark-eyed face seemed one of the most terrible things she'd ever perceived. It was fiercely angry.

"Thief!" the angry people around her started to clamour.

The dark-eyed stranger who had grabbed her arm said nothing, but just stared at her with his sombre eyes. Beth understood that upon an ordinary day those dark eyes would have seemed fine looking to her, but at this moment they were simply frightening.

"Master, methinks we should call the guards to deal with this!" a short man in the crowd tossed out.

There were many furious mutters of assent, and Beth searched for words to defend herself, but she found none. The people in the crowd were right, weren't they? She was now a thief. Even if it had been just a brief moment of weakness, for that moment she'd truly thought of stealing this man's purse. And this man wasn't even a rich, fancy lord like the knight who coveted her body, but, by the looks of it, just an honest, hard-working craftsman as her father had been.

The dark-eyed man glared at her.

"Nay, I think I'll deal with this myself. Right now," he said in a grim, gruff voice, as he began to drag her away.

Beth had no choice but to follow, accompanied by those people in the crowd who'd perceived what was going on. She tried not to picture what the stranger had in store for her. But when he dragged her to the stone steps of a house which overlooked the Square, she couldn't help but call out in fear.

"Wait… I…"

"You'll learn your lesson," the stranger cut her off in his grim voice.

"Aye, teach the thieving wench a lesson!" the voices of the onlookers clamoured in assent.

The stranger sat himself on one of the steps, dragging her

after him. What went on after that passed in a daze. Stunned, Beth soon found herself draped over the stranger's lap, with her skirts hoisted, her right arm pinned behind her back, and her bottom bared in front of all to see. She blushed with deep shame, trying to keep bitter tears at bay. There was no doubt as to what would follow. And it did.

Beth had already braced herself for the first spank which would land upon her bared bottom, yet the sheer sting of it took her breath away. The dark-eyed stranger had a big rough hand which, Beth soon understood, could do better work than even a stick or a belt. And it was plain he knew how to use it, because after only a couple of moments Beth's whole rump started to feel as if it was sizzling. The searing force of this hand was unbearable, and it seemed to know how to cover every inch of Beth's bottom and upper thighs. At first, she attempted to count the spanks the stranger landed upon her, in order to take her mind off the infernal sting the punishment was building there. But soon she simply lost count, and she began to sob in deep pain and humiliation. It hurt just like a brand of fire. Never in her life had she thought a hand spanking could hurt so much.

Right at the moment she thought the fiend who was punishing her would never stop, he blissfully paused, resting his roughened hand upon her poor scorched behind. She nearly opened her mouth to thank him, through bitter tears, for having stopped. And at that same moment she felt a strange, throbbing heat within her belly and sex. She swiftly pushed it away, as the voices in the crowd laughed and clamoured, asking for further punishment.

"Shall we fetch a birch for you, Master?"

"Perchance to add stripes to this comely thief's crimson behind?"

She bit hard into her lip, trying to still her sobbing. A birch? After the hard hand spanking she'd received, the sting of the birch would be beyond unbearable. More laughter and words from the onlookers followed, while she waited with a thumping heart, keenly feeling the throbbing pain in her punished behind. Would the stranger heed the onlookers and have a birch fetched to add to her punishment?

Deep relief coursed through her veins as she heard her punisher's gruff voice speak, "I think not. My hand will suffice."

Beth's relief was soon replaced by deep distress, because the hand resumed its spanking, bringing new, even more searing pain upon her poor scorched rump. He couldn't go on for eternity? Could he? In truth, Beth wanted to beg for mercy, but words seemed to have deserted her. Instead, she simply sobbed. She was still pitifully weeping when she belatedly realized her punisher had stopped at last, covering her bottom with her skirts, and allowing her to get off his lap. Yet she was now unable to get off on her own, and he had to help her scramble to her feet.

For a while, Beth hopped from one foot to another, in a vain attempt to alleviate the scorching sting in her bottom, but then she became aware that the crowd was finding deep entertainment in her strange dance. She stood still, simply hanging her head in shame. At this moment, she found she didn't even care what would further happen to her. She was too shaken by what had taken place.

"Look at me, woman," her punisher's stern voice rang in her ears.

She had no choice but to obey his command, fearing what would happen yet again if she didn't.

"Do you think you've learnt your lesson?" he asked her, perusing her with his dark eyes.

She nodded, and then lowered her gaze, loath to look in the eye of the man whose big, shovel-like hand had been, just moments before, setting her bare bottom on fire.

Her punisher heaved a resigned sigh.

"I hope it was indeed a lesson well learnt," he added in his deep voice.

She nodded again, feeling a shameful burn in her cheeks which nearly matched the one she felt in her reddened behind. Around them, she could hear laughter and approving exclamations from the crowd who'd witnessed her humiliation. When she dared to raise her eyes she saw her punisher was glaring upon the onlookers.

"There's nothing further to gawk at. The wench has been punished for her deed. And that's the end of it," he spoke, letting his dark eyes roam over the people who were still lingering.

To Beth's surprise the people gathered around started to disperse, heeding the dark-eyed man's command. Who was he? A craftsman whose word held weight, no doubt. She gulped nervously, as she was trying not to fidget on her feet and start rubbing her blazing bottom. Would this man now call the guards upon her and let them take her away? And what would her further punishment be? Would they use the iron brand and mark her face after they flogged her? Or even worse… She squared her shoulders, attempting to look the dark-eyed man straight in the face, and knowing she'd brought all this upon herself due to a moment's weakness.

She was well aware her eyes were still brimming with tears of pain and humiliation, but she tried not to flinch when the stranger's big hand took firm hold of her arm and started dragging her away from the Square. When she hesitated to follow, his other hand came swiftly upon her scorched behind forcing her to comply. He swatted her bottom mercilessly, forcing her to fall into step with him as they drew away from the hustle and bustle of the Square, and into the maze of streets that was the city of London. Beth tried to keep herself from succumbing again to flowing tears as she was forced to take this walk of shame. Her bottom stung fiercely, although at this time the hand had blissfully ceased its punishment, because she had fallen into step with her captor, striving to keep up with his long strides.

He stopped only when they'd reached an isolated lane, where there were no passers-by. Yet he was still holding her firmly by the arm. Beth could not help sniffing, pitifully, as she looked again into his very dark eyes. She'd expected to find searing anger in their depths, just as before, but at this time she perceived something different mirrored there. It was as if his dark gaze had softened upon her. She lowered her eyes again, unable to bear this new gaze, and, yet again, experiencing a strange, ignoble stab of heat in her belly. With blinding clarity, she understood that under different circumstances this big, strong man, with his black hair and his very dark eyes, could have taken her fancy. He was a man she'd have turned her head to stare after if they'd crossed paths on an ordinary day. But this was no ordinary day…

"That was an ill thing you did, wench," the stranger spoke, and Beth could do nothing but nod, in utter shame.

"Look at me when I'm speaking to you!" His gruff voice forced her to instantly comply because she feared his big hand would want to resume its punishment.

She knew her cheeks were flaming and her eyes were still watery, but at this moment there was no choice but do as the stranger wanted.

"Good," he said gruffly.

To her utter surprise, he let go of her arm. For an instant, Beth resolved to bolt, yet she swiftly changed her mind. She had brought this upon herself, and running away now would only add cowardice to her guilt. She might have unwittingly become a thief, but she'd never been a coward.

She squared her shoulders further and tried to meet her captor's gaze unflinchingly, although she became even more aware of the deep heat in her belly and nether parts when she looked upon him. It seemed not only his big hand, but also his coal-black eyes had the ability of setting her body on fire. What the dark-eyed man did next astounded her to her core.

"Here," he said.

With widened eyes, Beth saw he was now extending towards her the very purse she'd tried to steal. She shook her head, beginning to fear he was making a cruel jest.

"I-I don't want it..." she stammered in a strangled voice.

"You do," the big man said quietly. "Otherwise why would you have tried to steal it from me?"

She shook her head, deeply ashamed.

"I-"

There were no words she could speak, and she decided she shouldn't try to tell him she'd been in desperate need and that she'd never done such a thing before. He would not believe her. Who would believe a thief's word?

"Just take it. I mean it. It's plain you've more need of it than I do."

His voice held no trace of mockery, and his eyes looked steadily upon her. She shook her head again and he sighed.

"Take it already," he commanded, and as if transfixed, Beth found herself willing to heed his order.

She tried to clear her head. She could still feel the hard spanking she'd received from the very hand which was now extending the purse. This man was casting a strange spell upon her. Instead of resenting him for putting a fire in her behind, she seemed willing to heed him, although she'd never been one of those women to cower in front of men.

"But if you take it, I want your solemn vow you will not ever try to steal from anyone again," the dark-eyed man added, casting her a measuring glance.

When she stared at him mouth agape, he told her with a shrug, "I will not ask for anything else in exchange for it, if that's what you fear. I'm giving my money away freely, and we need not set eyes on each other ever again."

Beth found her voice with difficulty.

"I-I tried to steal from you. And now you... Why?" she babbled, thinking now it was all a dream and soon she would wake up in a grim gaol, to serve her punishment for what she'd attempted to do.

The dark-eyed man shrugged.

"It is only money," he said in an unconcerned voice, which made Beth twist her mouth into a bitter line.

He was obviously well to do and money didn't mean much to him. While she'd been desperate and starving, and ready to sacrifice her life over a purse of coins. Suddenly, her present humiliation hurt just as much as the fresh wound over the death of her mother.

"I want nothing from you," she shouted, knowing it was foolish pride, but unwilling to stop herself from uttering the words.

Yet the dark-eyed man didn't give her a chance to turn her back on him. He swiftly took hold of her arm and forced the purse into her hand.

"It's either this or I'll have you back over my knee and deliver an even harsher lesson than earlier. So what's it going to be?" he said in return.

Beth found her cheeks blushing even more fiercely than before, and that strange, treacherous heat mixed with distress taking hold of her. She went over the spanking in her mind, and felt the sting in her bottom tingle even more mightily than before. He couldn't spank her even more harshly than before? Could he? Again, she tried to clear her head.

"Do you wish for another spanking, woman?" the dark man asked her with an arched eyebrow.

Mutely, she shook her head, beginning to think she'd met a man who was out of his wits. He'd spanked her for trying to take his money. And now he was threatening to spank her for not wanting to take it.

"Good. Then have it. And I'll take my leave of you," he said, abruptly letting go of her arm.

Stunned, Beth stared after him as he turned on his heel. She searched hard for words to call out, but there seemed to be none. When she finally resolved to speak, she found he was already turning the corner of the lane. Bitter tears came to her eyes, now fully flowing, and she quickly wiped them off with the sleeve of her gown. She should thank God Almighty, and she should head home where she had her sad task ahead of her. She would give her mother the proper burial she deserved and then… She squared her shoulders knowing she would forever keep the vow the stranger had required of her. She would never even think to steal again. And she meant to find out who he was and pay him back every coin.

TOM WALKED AWAY with a faint smile on his lips, still shaking his head. Perhaps the beautiful thief he'd left behind would never learn her lesson, although he'd done the best he could. He doubted she fully realized it, but he'd delivered the spanking out of kindness rather than revenge. The people in the crowd had already been clamouring for the guards, and he'd had to act fast, taking the matter into his own hands. He'd reasoned a swift punishment from him would appease the furious crowd. He knew only too well punishments for thievery were harsh. A flogging or the stocks was the least the beautiful thief could have expected from the guards. So she should count herself lucky he'd taken the matter into his own hands and only reddened her luscious behind.

As he was heading home, he mused over the spanking he'd delivered, feeling his rod go hard and biting into his lower lip. He'd resolved to deliver a stern lesson meant to satisfy the angry onlookers and make the thief's bottom sizzle, but he'd not expected the thief to have such a scrumptious behind. Nor had he expected to feel such heat as he'd delivered the punishment in the crowded square. A punishment was a punishment – and there should have been no enjoyment about it – yet…

Tom frowned in puzzlement. It was probably because the thief was the most lust-worthy creature he'd ever set eyes upon. High perky breasts overstretching the fabric of her gown and a plump, well-rounded bottom. Auburn hair tinged with a bit of red and blue-green eyes which held a mixture of sultriness and innocence in them. He let out a wistful sigh. And he was not going to set eyes on her ever again.

As was his habit, Tom resumed work at the Forge as soon as his hurried repast was done. There was much ahead of him, and he did not have a moment to spare. He worked in silence for a while, but it seemed his other apprentices had been appraised by Micah, who'd been in the Square, of his encounter with the beautiful thief.

They were shy to ask questions at first, but then couldn't contain their curiosity.

"Micah says you really taught that thieving woman a lesson," Declan, the oldest of his apprentices, ventured with a wicked gleam in his green eyes.

Like all Irishmen, Declan loved laughter and teasing, and Tom had never begrudged his apprentice his sunny nature, but this time he found himself answering sharply.

"Better mind your work, lad," he barked.

Declan heaved an impudent sigh, but he had sense enough to mind his master, so the work took place in near silence for the next few moments or so. Yet soon the lads started whispering among themselves, and Tom heaved a deep sigh as he set his hammer down.

"Fine. Ask away, whatever you want and we'll have the end of the story. But after that we'll be done and over with, and you'll mind your work and be diligent about it. Understood?" he tossed out.

Micah, William and Declan all nodded with eager faces.

"Is it true you let her off without calling the guards, as Micah says?" William ventured.

Tom nodded with a grunt as he was studying his handiwork.

"Is it true she was as beautiful as an angel?" Declan cut in with a smirk in his voice.

Tom glared at him, yet he couldn't fully hide the half smile which appeared on his lips as he recalled how the woman's lush body had felt when it had been draped over his lap and he'd delivered the punishment.

"Nay," he answered after a while. "She was not as beautiful as an angel."

It was the truth. The woman was certainly beautiful, but there was nothing angelic about her. To him she'd looked more like Eve or even like Lilith, rather than like an angel from above. All flesh and blood and *all* woman. He realized he'd never been as tempted in his life by a woman as he'd been by the thief. That was probably why he'd let himself be fooled into giving her his money. He assumed he'd been foolish enough to let himself succumb to her charms. Yet, in truth, he'd not let her have the money because of her comeliness. There'd been deep sadness and despair about the woman he had perceived. Something heart breaking in her eyes, which had prompted him to want to aid her. But perhaps it had been all just an act. He shook his head with a shrug, deciding it was no use regretting what he'd done, and resolving to put the beautiful thief away from his mind.

"Now that we've all finished dreaming about beautiful women, perchance we can resume our work," he told his apprentices with an arched eyebrow.

Still, the boys seemed to be burning with curiosity, and Micah soon began to regal them with a retelling of the harsh spanking their master had delivered in the Square.

"I wish I could have seen that," Declan declared, apparently oblivious to Tom's glare.

Micah preened, for once happy he'd been party to a thing his older friend hadn't witnessed. Tom resigned himself to their talk, now returning his mind to his anvil. He studied the emerging lines of the sword he was fashioning, sighing within himself and knowing the knight who would bear it would not be worthy of its beauty. Tom would be loath to part from the sword, yet the knight had already paid coin for it – the very coin he'd given away. He looked at the sword, dismissing the thought of money, because, to him, money meant nothing at all compared to his craft.

It was only that evening that he came to think upon the money again, when Micah spoke to him during their meal.

"Master Tom, you'll have to give me coin to buy the fare for our table for this week," Micah said, as they were all finishing the gruel William had made for them this evening.

It had been William's turn to cook and, while he was better than both Micah and Declan at it, all of them missed Mistress Webb's cooking. Mistress Webb had cooked and kept house for them during these past three years, but for two months now they'd been left without her help, as she had gone to live in York with her married daughter.

"Coin," Tom muttered, striving to recall if there was any money left in the house apart from the purse he'd had with him this morning.

"Aye, coin!" Micah nodded expectantly.

Tom scratched his head. Even though he was very capable at the Forge and probably one of the most able smiths in the city of London, he was always loath to concern himself with money. Yet, studying the boys' still hungry and eager faces, he understood he was not doing a very good job of tending to his business.

"There are several people who still owe us coin for our

work," he said with a frown, fully knowing he should have kept a better tally of his customers and of his expenses.

He belatedly recalled there was, after all, some money left in one of his locked chests, so he rose, fetched it, and counted the coins out to Micah.

"Here," he said. "That should take care of this week's meals."

Micah nodded, but not before giving him an incredulous look.

"Er Master Tom. What of the purse you had with you this morn?" he ventured timidly.

"Never you mind," Tom muttered, waving his hand, but knowing the boys would be whispering among themselves as soon as he left the kitchen.

He went to bed with a deep sigh and a frown upon his face. Tomorrow he would have to sort out loose ends and collect what he was owed by those customers he'd been too lenient upon. He and his boys needed money not only for household expenses, but also for Forge supplies. Yet, instead of concentrating on this tedious task or of thinking upon his work, as was his habit, he found himself smiling faintly, and picturing the beautiful thief he'd spared from the guards. He pictured himself further reddening her luscious behind, and fully recalled the delicious heat of her scorched skin he'd felt under his palm.

Cursing under his breath, he began to pleasure himself, stroking his stiff cock with hard, hurried movements. He thought not only of the beautiful thief's reddened, scrumptious bottom, but also of her lush lips and of how those full lips would feel around his cock when she took him in her mouth. He fiercely climaxed while picturing her swallowing his sticky seed. After he cleaned himself, he resolved to find a woman willing to bed him as soon as possible. His arrangement with Sarah Webb had been satisfactory for both of them, but she'd been gone for two months. She was a widow, ten years older than him, and had been willing to share his bed while she took care of cooking and housekeeping. She was well liked in the parish and respected, so people had turned a blind eye to their arrangement, since Sarah Webb was already thought to be past her prime. He'd been sorry when she'd decided to join her married daughter in York, but other than a convenient arrangement for both of them, there'd been nothing he and Sarah had shared in truth. He had an inkling Sarah was well able to find a new husband for herself in York, should she ever choose to. Whereas he... well, everyone knew Master Tom Reed would not be able to ever find himself a wife.

CHAPTER 2

Beth stared around her, taking in the disorderly, dusty state of the kitchen she was in. While not downright grimy, it was in dire need of a good dusting and scrubbing, so she soon donned the apron which she saw hanging by the door and proceeded to the task at hand.

As she always did, she began to hum to herself as she worked, thinking upon the events which had brought her here. Master Tom Reed's house. Tom Reed who was a blacksmith just as her father had been. Brushing a loose tendril of hair off her forehead, Beth began to reason that maybe her encounter with Tom Reed hadn't been entirely random. Maybe the angel who guarded over her fate from above had made the encounter happen. It had set Master Tom Reed in her path when she'd needed his help. And, by the looks of it, Master Tom Reed was also in some need of her help.

It hadn't been that hard to find out who the dark-eyed stranger in the Square was. She'd been careful not to ask too many questions, or to venture in that area where people might recognize her as the thief who'd been punished. London might be a big city, but gossip and rumours travelled fast. News of the spanking a certain master blacksmith had delivered had spread after all, and it had taken Beth less than two weeks to find out her punisher's name.

As soon as she'd found out his name, she'd searched out his house, set on having a talk with Tom Reed and of assuring him she would find a way to pay him back the coin she'd spent on her mother's burial and on alms for her family's souls. She'd used the rest to pay what she owed for lodgings, which hadn't left her with much. She intended to use the little that was left to make a new start elsewhere – a town which might prove kinder to her than London or Winchester had been. But before she left, she had wanted to make sure the master blacksmith knew she intended to repay her debt.

Beth had knocked on Master Reed's door, yet she hadn't found him at home. Instead, an apprentice called William had let her in, telling her she could wait for Master Reed if she wished. Apparently unconcerned he'd let in a stranger, William had left her alone in the house, going back to his own tasks. And now Beth had resolved there was already a way to repay at least a small part of Master Reed's generosity. The kitchen, and, for that matter, the whole house was in sore need of tidying, and Beth had never been a woman to shirk from work. The state of the house had plainly told her that Master Reed had no one reliable to do the housekeeping for him, and a thought had firmly sprung in her mind. Their paths must have crossed for a reason. And it was plain there was a means to fully repay her debt sooner than she'd thought.

It was perhaps an hour later that she heard noises behind her as she was scrubbing the floors, and she rose from her task. She found Master Reed standing in the doorway with a look of sheer astonishment in his very dark eyes. Beth was more mistress of herself than last time, and she attempted to stare at him dispassionately, yet as soon as she let her gaze roam upon his form she recalled the way she'd lain defenceless across his lap while his big hand was punishing her bottom. She bit hard into her lip, trying to chase the image from her mind. Master Reed's dark eyes were blazing when they looked upon her, and, for a moment, Beth found herself thinking he'd take her over his knee right then and there to deliver that harsher lesson he'd threatened.

"What are you doing here?" Master Reed barked, his dark eyes aglow with anger.

This time Beth was able to find her voice.

"I've come to repay my debt," she said, trying to sound calm and composed.

There was a brief silence before he decided to speak and it seemed to Beth that Master Reed's dark stare was no longer blazingly furious. Although his voice was fully angry when he spoke.

"Leave! Now!"

"I've come to repay my debt," Beth repeated, struggling to make her voice not quiver.

She already knew Master Reed had a fierce temper. But she also recalled he'd helped her when she'd been in need. So she reasoned the worst she had to fear from this man was another spanking, and she also reasoned a spanking was something she could bear. Although...

"This is my home. You've no right to be here. And you've no right to meddle with any of my belongings," Master Reed snarled at her as he closed the distance between them in two large strides.

Beth strived to appear unconcerned when he took hold of her arm. But the moment his fingers came into contact with her flesh, Master Reed's dark eyes seemed to become warm and liquid, and that treacherous heat took hold of her whole body again as she glanced at him. They stared at each other mutely. And, at that moment, Beth understood one thing plainly. Master Reed also felt the very same heat she did. He felt that same maddening blaze in his own body whenever he looked at her. It was just like that between them.

He abruptly let go of her arm. His voice didn't sound angry, but weary when he spoke to her.

"I told you I want nothing in return. I gave that money away freely. You should leave now."

Beth hesitated for an instant. A part of her was telling her to fear the heat that clung between her and this man. Yet she'd never been a coward. So she decided to face that fear.

"I can work it off… My debt. By the look of this house, you sorely need someone to keep it for you."

He shook his head gesturing to the door.

"I want you gone. Now. Gone from my house."

The tone he spoke the words in was cold as ice, and Beth nearly shuddered. She was a stubborn woman, yet it was plain this man wanted nothing to do with her. She suppressed a sigh, understanding he might have helped her escape a grim fate, yet he probably believed her not only a thief but also a liar. What man would want such a woman in his house? Even a man as generous as Master Reed? She got a grip of herself, trying to quench the sudden pain which seized her heart. It was strange pain, because she barely knew this man, so she should not care what he thought of her.

"Good day to you then, Master Reed," she said, striving to make her voice appear as unconcerned as before. "I shall send the money I owe you as soon as I am able to."

She didn't wait for him to answer, and simply let herself out.

Tom cursed under his breath viciously. He'd come back home from his errands just to look upon the plump, luscious form of the beautiful thief he'd never thought he'd see again. The beautiful thief. In his home... And his first impulse had been to come upon her and hoist her skirts and have her right then and there roughly upon the floor. It had taken a mighty effort to restrain himself.

He stared after her as she stepped out into his yard, puzzled she'd come to seek him out. Was it true, what she'd said? That she really wanted to repay her debt? Or maybe she thought him a fool she could further deceive into giving her more money.

He shrugged, trying to tell himself he should not care. He wanted nothing more to do with this woman, and he should put behind him the blazing lust he felt for her. Still he couldn't help staring longingly after her, letting his gaze roam over the lovely swish of her hips, and recalling only too well how her plump behind had felt under his hand when he was spanking her.

It was then he saw another was also staring upon the woman with open, undisguised lust, and he found himself hating the predatory gaze of the man who'd come into his yard. It was Sir Lambert, the lord knight who'd commissioned the sword from him and who'd come to test it himself. Tom narrowed his eyes. He disliked both Sir Lambert and the way the nobleman was now gazing upon the woman who had suddenly stopped in her tracks.

To him, the way she'd suddenly paused didn't seem right, just as the way Sir Lambert was staring at her, and the satisfied smirk on the knight's face, didn't seem right. Without thinking, Tom strode out of the house to stand by the woman's side.

"My Lord," he said stiffly, making a minimal bow to Sir Lambert. "Your sword's ready. If you could step inside my shop I will show it to you."

Sir Lambert didn't seem to take in Tom's words. Instead, he cast savage eyes upon the woman. When Tom's gaze fell upon her, he saw her face was pale and her lips pursed. By the way both the woman and Sir Lambert were looking upon one another, Tom understood they were already acquainted.

"Sir Lambert, the sword!" he called in a commanding voice, not liking, at all, the paleness in the woman's face.

As if roused from a dream, Sir Lambert finally deigned to focus his gaze upon Tom.

"Ah, Master Blacksmith," he muttered in heavily accented English, then suddenly glared. "How did you come to know this woman?"

Tom hated the contemptuous tone in which the lord knight spoke the words, and saw the woman stiffen at the sound of the knight's voice. He also saw she was gazing at Sir Lambert with a look of undisguised contempt in her eyes.

"Sire," Tom said in Norman, which he'd learnt to speak quite well, in a tone that was pleasant but firm. "With all due reverence to your station, this is my own business."

Sir Lambert shook his head and now his predatory eyes glinted with sheer malice.

"You may not know, but she is a harlot."

Tom saw the woman flinch as the knight spat the word, and he found himself recoiling from it at the same time as she did. He made his tone even firmer when he spoke.

"My lord, you are mistaken. This woman is no harlot. She is my serving woman."

Sir Lambert widened his eyes in astonishment, but, before he could open his mouth to speak, Tom turned to talk to the woman, who was now gazing upon him with a look of astonishment of her own. He spoke sharply.

"Don't you have business scrubbing the floors?"

It took only a moment's hesitation, but he saw, with relief, she nodded.

"Yes, master. I'll get to my business at once."

"Mind that you do," he tossed at her, making his voice dispassionate and stern.

He held Sir Lambert's eyes as the woman retraced her steps to the house, not letting the knight follow her with his feral gaze.

"My lord, the sword?" he inquired, keeping his tone as firm as before.

Sir Lambert had no choice but to follow him inside the shop at the front of the house, where Tom had William fetch the sword for the knight to appraise and test. It was certainly a fine sword, and Tom had lovingly made it and carefully tempered its brittleness.

Sir Lambert frowned upon it, and Tom knew at once the lord was going to find fault with the sword. Of course Sir Lambert no longer cared about the sword. His thoughts must be all upon the woman he lusted after.

"Shoddy work, Master Blacksmith. Although, I've been told you make the finest swords in London."

Tom shrugged with a faint smile. He cared too little for Sir Lambert's thoughts upon him to take offense.

"I gather you do not want the sword then, my lord?" he said in an unconcerned voice.

"Of course I don't. It's ill-made, can't you see?" Sir Lambert shouted and placed the sword down, and Tom knew too well the knight would demand back the coin he'd paid two weeks ago for the sword.

"Ill-made?" Tom asked in a level voice. "Perchance for you. Lord De Brunne saw it a day ago and offered me twice your price for it."

Tom always spoke the truth, and in this case the truth was Lord Tristram de Brunne – the best swordsman at King Henry's court – had seen Tom's sword and taken a liking to it. He had indeed offered twice the price Lambert had paid, but Tom never went back on a bargain, so he'd declined De Brunne's offer. But now Sir Lambert no longer wanted the sword.

"My lord, since you find my work ill-made, I'll have your coin returned later today, when Lord De Brunne gives me the money for it. I'll sell it to him for the same price you paid, because it would be unfair to make him pay twice the coin another knight was willing to give me."

Sir Lambert's mouth was already curled into a snarl, and his fists clenched in impotent fury. Tom suppressed a smile, knowing Sir Lambert would hate that another lord, more esteemed than he was, would get what should have been his.

"I'll have the sword though, ill-made as it is," Sir Lambert hissed.

Tom shook his head.

"Nay, but you can't. You said it yourself you find it ill made. And I always strive to keep happy the lords who seek my services. I wouldn't want you to be unhappy, my lord. So, rest assured, I'll send my boy, Declan, later today with the coin you paid."

"Perchance I want my coin back now!" Sir Lambert snarled, understanding at last the sword was forever lost to him.

"But you shall have the coin. Today," Tom said, beginning to toy with the sword and rising himself to his full height.

Sir Lambert was a tall man, yet Tom was a head taller and broader of shoulder. And he might not be a knight, but he was skilful with a sword. One didn't learn to make such a weapon without knowing how to wield it. And soon Sir Lambert was no longer uttering anything, but just staring at him in impotent fury.

"Today, you shall have your coin, my lord," Tom repeated in flawless Norman to the furious knight, in a voice he made cheerful and unconcerned.

When Sir Lambert was finally gone, Tom allowed himself to let out a heartfelt sigh. A lord knight's hatred was the last thing he needed. Yet now he had it, and he had to thank the woman he'd spanked in the Square for it. After he'd instructed Declan what to do and entrusted him and William with the sword, he reluctantly headed to the house, knowing he and the woman whose name he didn't even know should have a proper talk.

~

BETH TRIED to still her thumping heart as she was trying to focus on the chore she was doing, but it was hard to keep the thoughts away from the man who'd been her doom in this city. She'd come upon Sir Lambert while she was at the Market, and ever since they'd crossed paths, the knight hadn't let her be. At first he'd been courteous and had tried to woo her, but Beth had seen his behaviour for what it was and she'd plainly told him nay. Sir Lambert might be handsome and a nobleman, but she'd had no wish to share her body with him, not even for the gifts and coin he'd been promising her.

She sighed out loud, recalling how Sir Lambert's attentions had prevented her from finding honest work and from gaining a living for her mother and herself in the city of London. It was as if a curse had fallen upon her, because it had been another man's lechery that had driven her away from her home in Winchester. In Winchester, the priest of their parish had spread vicious lies about Beth, claiming she'd attempted to lure him into sin. And in London, the knight who wished to have her had already told all and sundry she was a harlot. Beth had never shied away from work and had always thought herself capable of making her own living, even with her father and brothers gone and her home lost to her. Yet Sir Lambert's lies had followed her wherever she'd gone. Even when she'd tried to take in washing or mending, no woman had been willing to hire her. She'd attempted to find work as a serving girl, but it seemed her curse followed her wherever she went. The master who'd deigned to employ her had propositioned her boldly since the first day of work, and she'd had to leave his employ. This had gone on wherever she'd sought employment. It seemed only men were willing to hire her services, and they expected an entirely different kind of service from the one she was willing to provide.

Beth now attempted to focus on her task and put bleak

thoughts away. Her luck must change somehow and she should work harder to find her path. She raised her eyes only when she heard footsteps behind her. Straightening herself, she turned to face the man who hadn't asked for anything in exchange for his help.

"What are you called?" Master Reed asked, perusing her with his piercing dark eyes.

"I am called Beth," she replied, and tried not to blush under his searching stare.

She then spoke out of turn, although it was silly of her to wish to say such a thing to this man, who must already think the worst of her.

"I am no harlot!"

Master Reed shrugged, apparently unconcerned with her words.

"Your conduct before you came upon me is no business of mine," he replied quietly.

Beth suppressed a bitter smile, telling herself it was of no matter. She would soon leave this place and seek her fortune elsewhere. Yet a splinter of ice pierced her heart because she pictured her life in a different town. Men like Sir Lambert and the priest in her parish were everywhere. And she was not as dim-witted as to not understand her own looks and forthright manner would attract them everywhere she went. It did not matter she'd not even shared her body with a man – people already believed what they wanted to believe.

"He is gone," Master Reed said in the same quiet voice as before, and they both knew he was speaking of Sir Lambert. "Yet, I've come to know him. He is not a man to give up so easily on what he wants."

Beth nodded. Sir Lambert had hounded her mercilessly and he'd been certain she would turn to him when left with no means of gaining her livelihood. He'd already tried to force himself on her once, and Beth felt certain that tonight he would seek her out to finish what he'd started. She needed to go away from London this very night. Unless…

"You already told him I was your serving woman. Even Sir Lambert cannot lay claim on a woman who's part of another man's household," she spoke, casting the blacksmith a steady look.

Master Reed raked a hand through his dark hair and said nothing.

"If you let me stay under your roof I will be able to pay off my debt to you. I've done the sums and in ten months I'll be in the clear, if you provide food and lodging. I am a hard worker. You shall not be sorry if you take me on," she pressed, knowing this was a better chance of making a livelihood than any she'd been given so far since she'd been forced to leave her hometown.

Master Reed returned her steady look.

"If I let you stay under my roof everyone will think you're my leman, no matter the arrangement between us."

Beth supposed she should be grateful he'd only used the word *leman,* but there was no disguising it. Just as there was no disguising the heat that clung between her and this man with his strong arms and his very dark eyes. Beth had always been forthright. She understood that, no matter what she did, if she stayed under Master Reed's roof that heat would cling between them and soon begin to burn to blazes. She thought Master Reed knew it just as well as she did. And at this time she resolved there was no escape from it. She shrugged and replaced the word *leman* with the coarse one Sir Lambert had uttered.

"Well then… better your harlot than his," she said squaring her shoulders and casting the man in front of her a bold stare.

Silence fell between them, but then Master Reed spoke with a shake of his head.

"Nay. I've never forced a woman to sell herself to me."

Beth knew there was no return from what she would say next. She supposed she was not a good woman and she would have to serve penance for her impious words and thoughts. Yet things were what they were.

"But I am more than willing. It should be plain to you. Just as it's plain to me you are more than willing," she said, attempting to speak boldly, like a woman already used to the pleasures of the flesh.

And she made herself close the distance between them, taking his hand in hers. It was a hard, rough hand she'd already had occasion to feel upon her bottom. She then did a thing which, she understood, she'd wanted to do ever since she'd set eyes on him this morning. She raised his hand and softly brushed her cheek against it. It was then she heard Master Reed curse softly under his breath as he caught her in a swift embrace. He kissed her hungrily, gathering her into his arms. Beth had been kissed before, but never like this. She felt simply dazzled and had a hard time collecting herself when he broke the kiss.

"I am mad to be doing this," he spoke, and it seemed to Beth he was speaking more to himself than to her.

He stepped back, then cast her a glance which was half furious and half hungry.

"If I let you stay on..." he began. "Then–"

With a thumping heart, Beth waited for what he had to say next.

"There will be no deceit between us. I shall always be truthful. And I expect you to be truthful in return," he spoke softly.

Beth found it easy to nod her acquiescence. She'd always been honest in her dealings and, apart from her moment of weakness in the Square, she'd never really done wrong.

"I'm not a harsh man, but I will not tarry to take you over my knee if I think your behaviour warrants it," he added looking at her pointedly.

Beth bit into her lip recalling only too well the punishment she'd received from him. It was not something she wanted to experience ever again, although there'd been a strange, heated feeling when the spanking had taken place. And after the spanking, she... Beth strived to push the punishment away from her mind, because at this moment she did not know how she felt about it.

"You'll see, I'll never give you cause for it!" she vowed, thinking to herself the punishment in itself could easily be avoided if he was not a harsh man.

Besides, Tom Reed already seemed to believe the worst of her and he would be relieved to discover she was other than he thought.

CHAPTER 3

That night the supper they all shared proved to be different in many ways from what Tom was used to. For one thing, Micah, Declan and William were all staring at the woman who'd joined his household, with looks of sheer rapture upon their faces. And Micah seemed to have indeed forgotten she was the very woman who'd attempted to steal his master's purse. Tom supposed it was not only because of the meal she'd prepared for them that the boys were looking upon Beth like that. Her face and body were the stuff men's dreams were made of. He supposed he was mad to set a temptress like that in the path of green, untried boys like his apprentices. He very much expected he would soon regret taking someone who looked and acted like Beth as his woman. Yet, strangely, he'd felt he didn't have much choice about it.

He suppressed a sigh, focusing on his food, which was the best he'd eaten in months. In spite of the little time she'd had to provide a meal for four hungry males, Beth had made delicious frumenty to serve with meat. In that at least, as far as her cooking was concerned, the arrangement between them was going to prove better than good. Tom strived not to focus upon the other part of their arrangement which would prove better than good. He already knew he and this woman would be a wondrous match between the sheets. He'd felt this the very first moment his lips had touched hers...

"More frumenty?" Beth inquired solicitously, and all three boys eagerly nodded.

Tom suppressed a smile knowing they would have been licking their bowls even if Beth's food had been the worst in the world. They were already besotted with her, and there was not much he could do about it.

The boys nodded their eager assent, and Tom felt as eager as they were for the table fare. Yet soon he found himself wondering if something even more delicious than their meal was soon awaiting him. Would Beth wish to lie with him already? He did not want to foist himself upon her, yet he found himself already fantasizing upon what it would be like to kiss those full lips again and caress those ample curves. And he soon found himself picturing so many more things he could do.

In autumn, spring, and summer, the boys made their bed in the loft above his shop, which is where they headed now. The place offered plenty of room for their pallets and belongings. That was where Tom himself and his younger brother had usually slept when their parents had been alive. It was only in winter that they sought the warmth of the kitchen. His parents had sadly passed away not long after Tom had gotten married, and Tom's eyes roamed over to the chamber he'd shared with his wife in the years they'd been together.

"Do you wish to lie with me tonight?" he asked boldly, turning to the woman who was now standing rather shyly behind him.

She blushed, yet her voice was level and her back straight when she answered him, "Aye."

He wanted her with a fierceness he'd never felt for any woman in this world, not even for his wife. And it was not only because she was so comely. There was something about her which simply set his blood on fire, and he couldn't understand what it was. He shrugged away this unsettling thought, resolving it was better not to dwell upon it.

"I vowed to be always truthful. If we share the bed, you must know I can never marry you," he said.

He searched for further words to speak to her, suddenly loath to utter his wife's name this night when he thought of sharing his bed with another woman.

"I will never marry you," he cautioned, laying emphasis on every word.

Beth cast him a steady glance.

"Certainly, I understand. Rest assured, it is the last thing I will ever expect from you. I'm grateful that..."

He shrugged her words away, and told her levelly, because she needed to understand how it would be between them, "It's not payment of any kind I'm seeking. And I'll not force you to lie with me if you don't wish it."

Whether she shared his bed or not, tongues would be wagging anyway and she'd already branded herself a loose woman in people's eyes the moment she'd asked to stay under his roof. Yet Tom would not take advantage of Beth's predicament if she did not want him in her bed.

She returned his level glance and spoke after a while.

"That maddening heat between us... You feel it too."

Her words were bold, yet entirely true, and Tom found himself smiling at her.

"Aye," he told her, reaching to touch her face and brush his fingers across her soft skin.

He was very famished for her, yet he would strive to slow down and prolong both her pleasure and his before they got to couple. It was plain from her words she would not shy away from coupling with him. There was no air of maidenly modesty about her, and from the way she'd spoken it was clear to him she'd shared her body with a man or even several before. He recalled Sir Lambert's spiteful word, but decided to put it away from his mind. What Beth had or hadn't done before she'd met him was not for him to judge, as he himself could hardly be called a saint. He only hoped she would be content with their arrangement and would not seek to deceive him or look for the company of other men. At this thought, he recalled another woman in his life and the thing she'd done, and tried to push her image away from his mind. It was not that hard to do so though, because the woman in front of him simply set his blood on fire.

Beth widened her eyes. This time, she did so as modestly as a maiden, as he boldly pressed his palm over her full breast, beginning to rub it in circles. By the way she was looking at him now, it seemed as if no man had ever touched her like this, but Tom smiled, understanding it was an act she now chose to put on. Plainly, she wanted to be playful on their first time together. And Tom found himself loving this playfulness, yet reminding himself he should be cautious with this woman.

Was she, after all, a cunning, deceitful creature seeking to take advantage of him? It was true she'd attempted to steal from him in the Square. Yet her eyes seemed true and her voice honest whenever she spoke to him. Or was it just a clever deception? Just as the coy, innocent act she was attempting to put on now as part of their love play? Tom decided it was too late to repent, he'd agreed to this arrangement. He threw caution to the wind and captured Beth's full lips with his, now pressing his body close to hers, and feeling her luscious breasts sweetly crushed against him. He kissed her long, both gently and hard, because he soon perceived she was one of those women who took great pleasure in having his lips against hers and his tongue within her mouth.

"So, this heat you speak of..." he asked lazily, at last breaking the kiss and yet again brushing his palm against her clad breast.

"Now that we've kissed, does it feel to be more or less than it was?"

~

MASTER REED'S voice was playful and inviting, and Beth had begun to wonder how it was that this man, who'd spanked her so hard, could speak and touch her so gently. He was plainly teasing her now, and a mischievous smile had blossomed on his lips.

"You know it's more. Even more heat now than before. You're only teasing me," she muttered.

He slowly slid a hand inside her gown and boldly cupped her naked breast. She blushed scarlet, because no man had ever touched her this way.

"Master Reed, I–"

Would it be good to tell him now that she was new to coupling? But Beth's thoughts became muddled as the heat of his hand against her naked skin seemed to rob her of all reason. He chuckled.

"I see you like to call me Master Reed. Yet, since I'll thrust inside you tonight, it might be best if you called me Tom. So call me by my name."

"Tom," she muttered, as Tom began to unashamedly tease her nipple.

"Take off your gown," he said lazily after a while. "I wish to taste what I have touched."

Beth found herself complying with what he'd asked. She strived to appear calm and make nothing of the fact she was unused to standing naked in front of a man. Tom perused her for a long while with his handsome, dark eyes before he took her hand to lead her to the bed. When he lowered her on the bed, Beth began to think he would soon claim her, but it seemed

Master Tom Reed was far more master of his lust for her than she'd thought.

She blushed crimson when he took her nipple in his mouth, yet soon forgot to feel ashamed of the deep pleasure coursing through her. She found she loved his mouth upon her breast, and everything else his clever mouth and fingers started doing to her.

Yet she was seized by deep astonishment and shock when he kissed his way down her belly to stick his tongue where no man's tongue had been before.

"Wait... I–"

But she could no longer speak. The velvet of his tongue was simply bliss against her quim and it soon found that secret spot she never thought a man would know about.

"Oh, here it is, and it tastes so sweet," he said, as if in echo of her thoughts.

As he started to suck upon it, Beth began to moan wantonly, forgetting herself, and soon caring only for the bliss which took hold of her. She peaked against his mouth, and for a while couldn't even recall herself. It was as if in a beautiful dream that she heard her lover's voice.

"Spread your legs wide for me, *dearling*. I want to find my own release."

She obeyed him, because at this time she'd have gone through all the nine circles of Hell and back for the man who'd given her such bliss. He was now on top of her, and had taken firm hold of her hips. And soon she felt his hardness, probing against her soaking wet folds. He then thrust inside her, and his cock was hard and large, stretching her painfully. She gritted her teeth against the pain, knowing from her mother and from her married friends it was natural for a maiden to feel such pain when she was deflowered.

~

THE WOMAN beneath him was so very tight, and Tom nearly spilled himself when deep, fierce pleasure coursed through his veins as he entered her in one thrust. Never before had he felt so enraptured when he'd thrust inside a woman. He smiled to himself, gazing into the eyes of his new lover, because he liked the look of a woman well pleasured under him. Yet it was not pleasure he saw in her eyes, but pain. He frowned, opening his mouth to tell her she should not act and feign her pain. He'd heard some men enjoyed this kind of love play, but he didn't. Yet the strained look upon Beth's face didn't seem an act at all. Her pain was true. Just as the maidenhead he belatedly understood he'd just breached had felt very true to him. She was a maiden. Or, better said, she'd been a maiden. Cursing under his breath, Tom simply withdrew his cock from her body, gritting his teeth against the deep wave of lust and regret that seized him. She seemed relieved he'd retreated, but the damage had been done.

"What did you make me do, you foolish wench?" he muttered under his breath.

He felt like shouting at her, yet he couldn't bring himself to do it, because he'd just taken her maidenhead and she must still be in pain from it. As she sat up to stare at him, his eyes fell on the blood that already stained the sheets. Not much, because she'd fortunately been wet and eager for him. Yet he'd thrust hard inside her, and at least some of her pain could have been helped if she'd told him it was the first time a man would be inside her. He wiped the blood on his cock with the sheet, striving hard to keep his anger at bay.

"Did you think to trick me into marrying you?" he gasped, still stunned that someone he'd treated fairly would be capable of such deceit.

She shook her head, and Tom saw, in some relief, that her face no longer looked pale and strained and her eyes were dry of tears. The pain had probably been swift and it must have already passed, now he'd retreated. He strove to ignore his stiff cock and the sheer lust which was still seizing his body.

Hurriedly pulling a shirt over himself, which did a bad job of concealing his hardness, Tom strode angrily away from the chamber. He felt like taking the woman over his knee and giving her the mother of all spankings just there and then. And while he fully intended to spank her for her deceit, this was hardly the time to do it. He spent his night on the floor of the kitchen, unable to get a wink of sleep and seething with anger. How could a night which had begun so well turn out to be so foul?

He rose at dawn, and by the movements he heard in the bedchamber he knew Beth was already pacing up and down. He thought, with grim satisfaction, her night had been just as sleepless as his. Her face looked pale and set when he opened the door, but he told himself he should spare her no pity. She had deceived him, although he'd warned her he would have no deceit.

"You're up, I see," he said in a terse voice.

She nodded and looked at him with eyes which seemed steady.

"I didn't reckon it would matter to you. That is… it's not what you think. I understood from the beginning you would never marry me. So I did not mean to trap you into marriage."

He raked a hand through his hair. Her voice sounded true, but at this moment it no longer even mattered. He'd done it. He'd taken her innocence. And he had made a virgin into his leman.

"Whatever your reasons, it was a foolish thing to do. Plainly foolish!" he said, making his voice harsh. "You've ruined yourself. With a man who cannot ever marry you."

He felt blazingly angry with her, and his anger grew even more when he saw her shrug, with an unconcerned expression on her face.

"You call it ruin. It's just my maidenhead though. But I

suppose in everyone's eyes this is the only worth an unmarried woman can possess. She's only virtuous as long as she has her maidenhead. No other thing matters," she told him and her own voice sounded bitter.

Tom forced himself not to ponder upon her strange words, but on what had taken place. She might not see it, but there was no return from this and no way in which he could do right by her.

"Perhaps you didn't understand and I should have spoken even more plainly. I cannot ever be your husband. And it is not only because I do not wish to marry you. It is because I already have a wife."

She stared at him.

"But…"

"I do not share my life with my wife. And never will. *Ever again*. But that does not change the way things are. You know, as well as I, that no man can undo wedding vows."

He waited patiently for her disappointed astonishment, but none came. He only saw her shrug.

"I see. You now live forever apart from your wife, but that doesn't mean you cannot choose to share your bed and house with another woman. I did not ask for more. I agreed to become your leman. Why would you think I'd ask for more?"

He glared at her, because she plainly didn't understand he'd have felt compelled to wed her if he'd been free. He might not be noble-born, but he had his honour. And he'd always held his honour dear. Beth had just made him dishonour himself.

"You deceived me," he told her in a stern voice, knowing he would have to teach his new woman a lesson in honesty.

"I did not mean to! I didn't think you'd care!" she countered.

"Then you already think too little of me," he replied in turn.

She heaved a deep sigh, and he narrowed his eyes at her.

"You've just become my woman and there is naught either of us can do about it now. Still, there is something that needs to be done. You need to be taught not to hide things from me as you did. You need to see that what you did was reckless. And I intend to deliver a lesson you'll remember well. A lesson for your own good."

His eyes challenged her to protest his decision, but she only sighed again.

"So I suppose you'll spank me for this… just as you told me you would."

"I am a man of my word," he told her tersely.

Her blue-green eyes seemed very uncertain when she looked at him, so he decided it was best to speak plainly.

"You shall be spanked tonight. And well spanked," he said in a steady voice.

She nodded with a fierce blush on her cheeks, and Tom supposed he should feel pleased by her acquiescence, yet he still felt terribly angry with both her and himself. There was no return from the course both their lives had taken, and she would have to learn what being his woman meant. Once she'd indeed learnt he expected full honesty from her, there'd be no further need of harsh lessons. Yet he knew it was a harsh lesson she needed to learn.

"I'm off to my chores," he called to her from the kitchen, when he was fully dressed.

Beth came to where he was, and looked at him in a level way. Her eyes seemed to hold no regret for the reckless way in which she'd ruined herself, but he promised himself he would teach her about recklessness tonight.

"I'll have lunch ready at noon," she called to him in a placating voice, but he turned his back on her, still angry about the way things had turned out between them.

BETH STRIVED HARD NOT to think upon Master Reed's promise of a good spanking, yet from time to time her thoughts drifted upon it. She thought of the spanking she'd already received from him, and of how sore and red her bottom had been for several days after. But she also thought of the strange, shameful heat she'd felt pulsing in her quim whenever she'd touched her reddened skin. And she also thought of the great pleasure she'd had whenever Master Reed's lips and hands had been upon her. It was mightily strange she didn't think upon a spanking from him only with distress. Nevertheless, she attempted to steer her mind away from the spanking, which, she understood, couldn't be avoided in any way.

Tom Reed had seemed set on his course, and it would be to no avail to plead with him she hadn't meant to deceive him. Because, in truth, she had ended up deceiving him, knowing deep down within herself that a man such as he was wouldn't have lain with a maiden. Yet, she'd fiercely wanted to be with him, in spite of all, and that was why she'd resolved not to tell him, lying to herself he would not set such great store on it even if he were able to tell. So he was right. She had, in a way, broken her word to him of always being forthright. And she'd managed to do so on the very first night spent under his roof.

She suppressed a sigh, returning her mind on the chores she had to do in a house which hadn't been tended properly in several months. She scrubbed and cleaned and put things to rights, at the same time keeping an eye on the potage she had boiling on the stove. She remembered too well Forge work was hard, and that at lunch the menfolk working there would be hungry and eagerly waiting for their food.

They were indeed hungry, she saw, as soon as lunchtime came and they came to seat themselves around the table. Beth watched with a suppressed smile the way the growing boys ate, suddenly feeling sad because the three brothers she'd lost one after the other in a mere week, had been only a little older than the boys in front of her. She bit her lip, striving to focus on the talk instead.

"Wait and see, I'll be a journeyman well before you!" Declan was now boasting to both William and Micah who must be a year or two younger than he was.

Beth stared into her bowl, attempting to hold back her tears as she recalled the pride and joy in her brothers' eyes when they'd gone from apprentices to journeymen. It had been a big step for them, as the Guild's members' standards were high in her hometown. She focused on the matter at hand and assumed these requests to be even higher in a big city such as London. To become a journeyman Declan would be required to have his master's permission to show the Guild members items of his own making.

As if in echo of Beth's own thoughts, Micah started teasing his friend, declaring that surely the esteemed members of the Guild would split their sides with laughter as Declan was unable to fashion even a horseshoe. Master Reed said nothing, just shaking his head and smiling. Beth already understood he must be very skilled, because she'd known of few town smiths able to wield fine swords. Her own father had never made weapons or armour, but it seemed Master Reed was also becoming known as a swordsmith in London, and lords and knights had already begun to seek his work, although he chose to reside within the city and not within castle walls under some nobleman's patronage. Beth already suspected a man like Master Reed would never seek the patronage of a lord. The disdain in his eyes over Sir Lambert had been clear for all to see.

At present, the apprentices continued their squabble over who would become the most able of them, and at last Master Reed stepped in with a cocked eyebrow.

"Seems to me of late you've all started daydreaming and are barely able to tend the fire in the Forge. As for the lessons I tried to teach, I wonder if you can remember them. And you, Declan, have your head in the clouds even more than these other two!"

Declan shook his head, his face a picture of innocence, though Beth had already started to suspect that, of all three boys, he gave the most trouble to his master and was the most mischievous.

"Not so, I swear. I already know the right and proper way to make an auger bit, just as you showed us last week!"

Declan then fiercely blushed as Master Reed began to look at him expectantly, and as Micah did not miss the opportunity to make a further taunt.

"Aye, Declan. Pray tell us… Since you're the best and oldest of us, you should indeed share your knowledge."

"Fine," Declan replied with a dignified tilt of his head. "I'll tell you then. For the bit to be made, the smith most surely has to hammer and grind that piece of iron into the shape he wishes…"

"Ha," Micah said with a wave of his hand. "Everybody knows that!"

A pointed look from Master Reed silenced him, and Declan was left to go on with the lesson he meant to share.

"And then…" he went on, but suddenly looked upon Beth and became rather flustered.

Beth understood that Declan might be a brash, mischievous boy, but she was a new woman in their household. She resolved to help him overcome his shyness.

"I reckon," she said with a shrug, as she began to ladle more potage into William's now empty bowl. "What Declan surely means to say next is that the iron then needs to be covered in fat. Stale fat, if I'm not mistaken, but I think some smiths also use burned bone for this part. Isn't it so?"

Declan nodded at her, yet his cheeks now burned even more fiercely. Still, he soon cleared his throat and regained his voice.

"Aye, it is just so. And then there's the kneaded clay you need to place it in. Then it goes into the furnace for the hardening of the case. And then, while it's red hot you plunge it into water–"

Here Micah could no longer hold his peace. "Aye, though some say it needs to be placed into the piss of a red-haired boy, to make it better!"

Both William and Micah started shrieking with laughter, and Declan's face got just as red as his hair. Master Reed smiled with good humour, and Beth suppressed her own smile, attempting to make Declan more at ease:

"That is a tall tale though, isn't it, Master Reed? I know some smiths swear by it, but I've never seen one use this in order to fashion an auger bit or any other such item."

Master Reed's dark eyes bored into her before he nodded.

"A tall tale, for certain, just as Beth here says. Water is what you need for quenching, but then the item will be somewhat brittle. So to remove some of the brittleness, it needs to be held over the fire for gentle tempering. An auger bit should be hard, yet not so hard that it should break when twisted sideways. So it's tempering it needs. But how does one know the bit's been tempered just well enough?"

"The colour of it!" all three boys hurried to answer, and Beth understood that in this, at least, they knew their lessons well.

"Just so," Master Reed nodded, then started to talk about more of the work they still had ahead of them today.

Yet Declan, William, and Micah seemed to have their heads in the clouds just as much as their master had said. They kept staring at Beth instead of listening to Tom Reed, and he soon ceased his talk with a sigh.

"Quit staring. It's not as if Beth here is the first woman you've ever glanced upon, is it?" he said, eyeing his apprentices with an arched eyebrow.

"Nay, Master," Micah muttered. "But it's plain *she* knows of smithing."

"Aye, it is plain she does," Declan muttered in his turn, then frowned at her in puzzlement. "How come you know so much of it?"

Beth shrugged, but she caught Tom Reed's penetrating gaze upon her. And she recalled she'd vowed to be entirely forthright with him and had already broken her promise once.

"My father was a blacksmith. I know my way around a forge."

"You said, he *was* a blacksmith. He no longer is one?" Declan asked, between slurps and mouthfuls.

Beth had already noted the boys ate like wolves, not minding their table manners. Master Reed also ate hungrily, yet it was plain he'd had a mother who had taught him proper ways. She sighed within herself, understanding he'd taken no pains to teach his apprentices their table manners and this was yet another chore that would fall to the woman who kept his house.

"My father is no longer among the living," she said, feeling fresh pain upon uttering the words, though her father had been gone for more than half a year.

"May God rest his soul," Declan muttered, and the others nodded.

"What of your other family?" Master Reed suddenly asked, perusing her with his penetrating dark eyes.

"Gone to Heaven, just like my father," she replied, striving to make her voice peaceful and serene.

Within herself, she still grieved for her family, and it was barely two weeks since her mother had passed. But in truth, her mother's passing had been a relief after those months of cruel suffering. Her mother's heart and soul had truly died when her husband and sons had been taken from her. And some months later her body had followed. Beth daily tried to tell herself her mother was now happy in Heaven, reunited with her beloved children and with her husband. At times, she'd thought it would be better if she soon joined them in the afterlife, yet she'd always been the kind of woman who looked forward to the sun shining in the sky and to the world around her. She still grieved for her family, yet she just couldn't bring herself to wish for death.

There was a small silence around the table, yet the boys soon resumed their chatter while Master Reed perused her with a softer look in his dark eyes which had been so flinty when they'd gazed upon her this morning.

"When did you lose your kin? Not long ago, I reckon. Your speech is different, and it doesn't carry at all the sound of London. You came to London when they died?" he inquired.

Beth nodded, loath to speak more of her troubles. She did not want him to think she would want to stir his pity with her sad story. He might not even believe she spoke the truth. It was plain he already thought her dishonest, and she hadn't made a good start of it last night.

"I see," Master Reed said, without pressing, and Beth was grateful he didn't.

Later, when the day was done at last, Beth busied herself clearing the kitchen after their supper. As soon as the boys had gone to the loft where they slept, she waited for Master Reed in the bedchamber with a thumping heart, her thoughts returning to the punishment he'd promised he'd deliver.

She glanced at him warily when he finally entered the bedchamber. Would he spank her now? She also thought of lovemaking and how she'd luxuriated under Tom Reed's caresses, but also of how she'd felt pain when he'd thrust inside her. She recalled what some of her married friends had said about lying with their husbands. Kisses and caresses from a man were pleasurable, when the man could be bothered to bestow them upon his wife, but it was never as pleasurable when a man thrust inside you. Some of her friends had even called this part of married life downright distasteful.

Beth bit her lip, not knowing what to think, and sighing at the thought of having her bottom sizzle under Master Reed's big strong hand. He strode to where she was, but said nothing, and to Beth the silence became maddening.

"Well, better to get it done and over with, I guess," she found herself saying, because she'd never been a patient woman. "I'm ready for the punishment, so you know, and will not try to talk my way out of it."

"It's good to know," Master Reed said in a calm, level voice, as he sat himself on the bed.

"Will you... will we... will we bed before or after the spanking?" Beth suddenly found herself blurting out, and Master Reed arched a dark eyebrow at her.

She cleared her throat, then went on, feeling her cheeks flame, "Because... I mean... We... you left in anger and I still don't know that much about it... And I..."

"Do you always prattle so much before a spanking?" Tom Reed asked her and there was a faint smile on his lips.

"I've not been spanked much," Beth confessed with a sheepish shrug.

"Hence the prattle," Tom Reed said drily.

"But you–"

He sighed, patting his lap.

"I'll spank you lightly, for a start. Then, if you wish, we'll finish what we hadn't had time to finish last night. Afterwards though, I mean to teach you a harsher lesson."

"Oh..." Beth found herself blushing even more fiercely.

Yet she obeyed him when he beckoned her, because she had vowed she'd submit to the punishment. Soon, she found herself lying over his lap, with her skirts hoisted and her bottom bared. She braced herself for the sting of the first spank, knowing from bitter experience it would hurt, because Tom Reed had the hands of a hard-working blacksmith.

Yet the first spank the master blacksmith delivered upon her bottom was light, and didn't sting at all, and so was the next, although it stung faintly. His large hand caught both her cheeks, but then he started alternating, spanking her left and right cheek in turn. The sting was faint, and Beth soon began to feel that strange, shameful pleasure in her belly, which built into a sweet ache that made her fingers and toes tingle. He was still spanking her, and his large hand was kindling a strange warmth all through her body, until her quim started pulsing and she understood she'd begun to mewl like a kitten. She bit into her lip, feeling her face go scarlet. What would he think of her? Behaving like a wanton when he'd begun to punish her? What if he became angered and started spanking her bottom as hard as he had that day in the Square? She gulped as Master Reed now delivered a sharp, stinging smack on that sensitive spot on the back of her thighs. And her quim simply gushed at the same time as she felt the scorching heat of the blacksmith's hand.

"Ah..."

She moaned wantonly, and found herself frowning when Tom Reed's hand paused spanking her, and started tending to her soaking wet quim. It didn't take much tending. Soon she found herself moaning in sheer rapture and climaxing against his clever fingers.

"So," Master Read said levelly, letting her slide off his lap.

Beth's knees already felt weak, and she didn't protest when he divested her of her gown and shift then lowered her on the bed, parting her legs.

"Let's finish what we didn't get to finish," he said softly, pulling his tunic over his head and then swiftly stepping out of his braies.

Beth widened her eyes, and gulped.

"Your..." Suddenly, she blurted out, because she'd never been a woman to know to hold her tongue, "It's good I didn't see it last night. I'd have thought you meant to shred me to pieces with it."

Tom Reed laughed, mischief dancing in his dark eyes.

"Are you trying to flatter me?"

She shook her head, telling him earnestly, "Nay. It's… Do you think it will fit again?"

He came above her, and settled himself between her legs.

"Never fear, I'll slide in gently. And I'll be mindful you're new to coupling. Besides, you're already wet and slick for me."

Beth nodded, now attempting to hide her doubt. True to his word, he didn't thrust in hard, as he had last time, but slid in gently. Beth closed her eyes and braced herself for the pain she'd felt last time, but none of it came, just a slight discomfort, which was soon replaced by pleasure as he started moving in and out of her.

"How about this?" he muttered, and his voice sounded somewhat ragged.

She encircled him with her legs, because she had already begun to want him deeper inside. He smiled.

"So… already getting used to me, I see," he said, in the same ragged voice, as he began to thrust harder and deeper, and caused Beth to moan in sheer delight.

Her friends who'd said this thing was not pleasurable had most certainly lied about it, Beth decided. But soon all thoughts were robbed from her head. Rapture conquered all her senses and her quim clenched convulsively around her lover as she shouted her joy. He still pumped hard within her for a while, and then he suddenly left her body, moving to spill his seed next to her on the sheet.

It took Beth a long while to come back to herself, and, when she did, she perceived he was looking at her with a shake of his head and a smile upon his lips.

"I didn't think you'd find your bliss so soon with me inside you… because you're so new to lovemaking. But it seems I was mistaken."

She frowned.

"Did I do something wrong?"

He shook his head, brushing an errant lock of hair from her face.

"Nay. Not at all. That heat between us seems even more powerful than I thought."

She nodded, but then she recalled what he'd promised her.

"Speaking of heat, you promised to further warm my bottom after we're done. Will you still do it now?"

"I promised that, didn't I?" Tom said in the same calm, level voice he'd employed when he'd vowed he'd teach her a harsh lesson.

Beth gulped, understanding only too well now that the earlier spanking had been just meant to tease. And she thought of the next spanking she'd receive, and her heart started thumping in both distress and curiosity. What did he mean to do next?

"MAYBE... DID YOU CHANGE YOUR MIND?" Beth asked in a hesitant voice, which sounded half hopeful and half doubtful.

Tom stifled a sigh. In a way he had. Because it seemed unfair to spank her after he'd taken her maidenhead only last night. And it seemed unfair to punish a woman who held such grief in her eyes when she spoke of her departed family. It was plain the grief was still fresh, and he knew only too well grief prompted people to be reckless. He'd thought upon things today when his searing anger had passed, and he'd reasoned Beth had spoken the truth and had not done what she'd done with the design to deceive him. She had been only reckless, not understanding she was changing the course of her own life by the reckless act. And now he understood why she'd behaved so recklessly. She was still grieving for her family. And grieving people didn't always think straight.

Yet Tom hadn't wanted to look like a man who didn't keep

his word and let his new woman get away with anything, because that would prompt further recklessness from her. So, from the beginning, he'd resolved to still spank her, but to do it in such a way that would be more like love play rather than punishment for both of them. He'd never done this before – given a spanking as part of love play – but he'd heard there were men and women who enjoyed this kind of play. And now that he had given a spanking as love play, he understood very plainly he'd not been the only one to find enjoyment in this mild, teasing spanking. Beth's wet, soaking quim after the spanking and her moans of rapture had told him what he needed to know. And blood now started pumping hard in his veins, because he understood their mutual enjoyment need not be over so soon. Besides, his new woman's recklessness need not go quite entirely unpunished.

"Nay. After all I have not changed my mind," he said, making his voice level.

"Oh," Beth said, and he loved it that she blushed crimson when he patted his lap.

"So you'll spank me hard now," she muttered, yet she obediently assumed the required position over his lap, and his cock stirred dangerously because it was very arousing to see her submit to his punishment.

"I'll spank you *harder.* Though not even half as hard as you deserve," he said, understanding he was already savouring the words on his lips.

He breathed in, trying to contain his arousal, knowing too well his hard cock was prodding stiff against her body, and that she was certainly able to tell. He rubbed her pink bottom in slow circles, and then spat in his palm, knowing his wet hand would sting more. He had no intention of spanking Beth really hard, yet he wanted her to feel the sting of his spanks and remember he could punish her much harder if she behaved recklessly again. He started with slow spanks, which first covered the crown of her buttocks, and then descended to pepper the back of her thighs. He didn't spank for long, yet he knew his hand was strong and steady. So Beth's lush behind was quite soon a good shade of red. She was already whimpering softly, and he understood she would be more comfortable sleeping on her belly tonight.

"So," he said softly, now resting his hand on her warm, reddened behind and loving the feel of it. "What lesson did you learn from this spanking?"

He put his other hand to work, now tending to that sweet spot between her legs, and noting with a smile that it was very swollen and that her quim was even more soaking wet than before.

"I..."

It was plain his woman had trouble speaking, and, in order to make her focus, he gave her a light swat that caught both her reddened buttocks.

"I shall never deceive you again," she said at last with a small sniff, in a voice that sounded delicious to his ears, because it was filled with both lust and contrition.

"And?" he trailed off, giving her a harder smack right on her sit spot.

"Ah... I... What else do you want me to say?" she added in a questioning voice.

"That you'll never behave so recklessly again!" he told her with a slight frown, because he was still astounded she didn't see that surrendering her maidenhead to him had been reckless.

"But I wanted you to claim me. It was my choice to make, not yours," she countered in a puzzled voice.

Tom now contemplated giving her a far harder spanking, because she plainly didn't understand she'd ruined her life. Yet he contented himself to lay just a couple of stinging spanks on her heated behind, promising her in a voice he made very stern, "You've clearly not learnt your lesson. But the next time I spank you, you will indeed, and I'm of a mind to cut a switch from that apple tree in the yard."

Yet the thought of the switch, and how he could use it, conjured up heated images in his head. He began wondering whether he'd not erred in bringing it up, because by the way Beth stirred over his lap, it seemed she was more aroused rather than afeared by the mention of this kind of discipline. He suppressed a sigh, promising himself to really punish his woman for her own good in the future, because it seemed plain he'd not managed to teach her anything tonight, other than how to enjoy their lovemaking.

"Off you go now, and mind what I've told you!" he said, giving her reddened bottom a light swat.

She obeyed him with a sniff, now moving to lie on her belly. Tom stretched out with a smile, picturing himself thrusting into her from behind and feeling the lovely heat of her reddened bottom against his front. Yet by the way Beth was now lying in bed, he soon understood she was tired, and he recalled she'd toiled hard today to put his house to rights and see to their meals. He'd been of a mind to tell her she shouldn't work so hard, as his needs were simple, and there was time enough to see to the house in the weeks and months which would come. He promised himself to tell her so tomorrow.

He cast a wistful glance upon Beth, who had already dozed off, plainly exhausted. As he lay on his own side of the bed, sleep soon started to claim him as well. Just before he went to sleep, Tom realized, rather hazily, that it was the first time in years a woman was sleeping by his side.

CHAPTER 4

Tom woke as usual, at the rise of dawn, and saw that Beth had already roused and was reaching for her shift and gown, which lay discarded on the floor, where he'd tossed them last night. As she was bending to pick the garments up, he perceived the delicious redness of her plump behind. It was only a faint shade of red, because he'd not spanked her hard last night.

"Good morrow to you. But who said you could get dressed?" he called.

She turned to face him, the pretty blush on her face surpassing, by far, the lovely hue of her behind.

"Oh, you're up then," she said, and her eyes soon fell on Tom's cock which was certainly stiff, as was its habit in the morning.

"Come here," he told her, with a smile. "We've unfinished business from last night."

She groaned, but Tom perceived she had a half-smile on her face. He reached for her and made her straddle him, liking the look of sheer wonder and delight in her blue-green eyes. When he reached between them, to touch her between her legs, he found she was already wet.

"We've no time for leisurely lovemaking. So I mean to be faster about this, though I vow you won't be complaining," he said, positioning her to his liking and taking one of her nipples in his mouth.

"Oh..." his new lover moaned eagerly. "But... I mean, like this? I don't know how..."

"I'll guide you," he replied, speaking against her heated flesh.

He was true to his word, soon showing her how to match the rhythm of his cock and sway her hips while she rode him. His new woman was a quick learner, and the lovemaking was fast, yet hot and pleasurable, and they both climaxed at the same time, while Tom's mouth was around her sweet nipple.

After they were done, Beth sat down next to him, rather gingerly, and he couldn't help but cast an eager look upon the way she was behaving after his spanking last night. He'd simply loved spanking her, and now he found himself also loving the thought of her pink, chastened behind.

"Still somewhat sore?" he asked her, savouring the question on his lips.

She nodded with a glare at him, and Tom couldn't help but grin broadly. He hadn't spanked her hard, and by tonight the pinkness in her bottom would subside.

"Good," he said, making his voice cheerful. "Although it's been far milder than you deserved and you already know it. Next time you step out of bounds I'll spank you harder," he promised and suppressed a big smile at the way Beth widened her blue-green eyes.

The look in her eyes now held a mixture of astonishment and resentment, but there was something more he saw mirrored there.

"You said you were not a harsh man." He heard her mutter, but her voice didn't hold true fear.

"And I am not. Yet as my woman you need to learn the

bounds of proper behaviour," he said, although at this moment proper behaviour was the least of his concerns.

Improper behaviour was what he had in mind. Such as renewed lovemaking in broad daylight. But he sighed, knowing his work could wait no longer.

Beth narrowed her eyes.

"Proper? I am your leman, remember?"

He found he didn't like the word anymore.

"You are my woman now," he amended. "Are you denying that?"

Beth shook her head.

"No, but..."

"Arguing with me, already?" He grinned, finding the perfect excuse to do what he'd intended all along, and of postponing his work a little longer.

In a moment, Beth was draped over her lover's lap, face down. Tom saw her brace herself for the searing touch of his hand falling upon her skin, but he'd already come to see she both feared the sting which would come and at the same time eagerly waited for it. He decided to be mischievous, and instead of swatting her behind, he began to rub it in tantalizing circles.

"A bit reddened from last night, but not red anymore," he murmured, lightly brushing his fingers over her skin and knowing his touch was adding scorching heat to her already heated sex.

He couldn't suppress a grin because when he stuck a finger inside her quim, he found her gushing wet. He struggled hard to keep his arousal at bay as he started further tending to her.

BETH HAZILY THOUGHT she'd never experienced sheer bliss until she had become acquainted to Tom Reed and his clever hands.

They were clever hands indeed, as they could bring both punishment and rapture. So much rapture.

"Christ above," she muttered when at last she came back to herself, then instantly regretted using blasphemous words.

Her lover didn't seem to mind. He just chuckled as he lowered her on the bed, propping himself on his haunches above her. He parted her legs and rubbed his engorged manhood against her soaking wet quim.

"Mm... well spanked from last night. Well-loved from this morning, yet still gushing wet. For me," he said, using words which made Beth blush to the roots of her hair.

Still, at this moment, she reasoned he could use whatever words he pleased after already giving her so much rapture. She understood he longed to thrust inside her again, yet she found him still hesitating, and he didn't enter her even when she parted her legs widely and thrust her hips invitingly towards him. Was she too new and artless about this?

"Am I doing this wrong?" she asked him in earnest.

He laughed.

"Nay. I want to thrust inside you to the hilt. Yet you're still new to lovemaking. And I loved you just moments before. I was just wondering whether you're not still too sore."

She glared at him.

"My bottom's still sore and you know it."

He sighed.

"So new to love play... and I keep forgetting. *Dearling,* I didn't mean your bottom, but your quim."

She still blushed scarlet as she shook her head. Still, he didn't enter her.

"You're certain, woman?" he muttered as his dark eyes glowed with undisguised longing.

Again she raised her hips to him, and this time he didn't spurn her invitation. He thrust inside her, and then he loved her more gently and more leisurely than he had before. Yet he was big and Beth keenly felt his hardness within her body, and soon she forgot even to think, as she succumbed to the sheer rapture of being loved by him. Tom climaxed just after she did, spilling his seed, just as before, not inside her, but on the sheets.

"When are your monthly courses due?" he asked bluntly, as he was wiping his cock with one end of the sheet.

Beth hesitated at first, but in view of what they'd already shared, she made herself answer. "At the beginning of next month. Why are you asking?"

She wasn't schooled in the ways of lovemaking, but she knew men didn't like women to speak of such things, and stayed away from a woman's bed while she was having her moontime. Yet she also recalled her mother had told her that missed monthly courses might mean a pregnancy, so she began to understand why he'd asked the question.

"But you didn't give me your seed," she said pointedly, also already knowing a woman couldn't conceive unless she received her lover's essence.

"I didn't," he nodded. "Yet I have not so much knowledge of such things. I heard it said a woman might sometimes find herself with child even if her lover withdraws from her body at the moment of his rapture. Perchance it would be better to keep a tight record of your courses. And I'll think of a woman you can speak to. Perhaps she will know how to advise you."

"Advise me?"

"Aye, I know for certain women use brews and herbs. And there is a thing such as a pessary you might inquire about," he told her as he was washing up in the water basin by the bed.

Beth recalled having heard the word spoken by the priest in her hometown, who'd said women who used such things risked eternal damnation. But she also recalled how that very same priest had tried to woo her after her father and brothers' deaths, and how he'd denounced her as a loose woman when she'd spurned his advances.

Tom obviously didn't miss her hesitation.

"This is one of the reasons I got angry that you hid your innocence from me. The lovers I took after I parted from my wife were all knowledgeable of such things, and I cannot advise you in women's matters. All I can do now is find someone who can. Neither you nor I are prepared to deal with a child out of wedlock."

She nodded, although there was a strange sadness which came upon her when he uttered the word *child*. She'd always wanted children and had expected to cradle sons and daughters in her arms when she wed. But now she understood she may never wed. So she may never have children.

"Do you have children of your own? Already?" she asked, trying to push the nagging thought away.

"No. None. Sons nor daughters... Not in wedlock and not out of it," Tom answered and his voice seemed tense and somewhat bitter as he spoke.

The words flew unwittingly, before she could call them back, "And did you never wish for children of your own?"

Tom had already fully dressed while they'd been talking. He stared away from her when she asked her artless question, just saying, "Have a care and clean yourself thoroughly, this time and every time after our lovemaking. I'm off to my chores, and I suppose you already know what yours are."

She didn't have the time to speak again, because he left the chamber hurriedly.

CHAPTER 5

As weeks passed, Tom had occasion to see Beth had not lied to him when she'd told him she was a hard worker. Every day she fulfilled her end of their bargain and he had naught to complain about regarding her housekeeping skills. Rather, he attempted to tell her he didn't need her to toil so hard for his comfort, yet she shrugged his words away. She still had it in her head to repay her debt to him, although he'd let her know he didn't think upon it as a debt. From his end, he'd tried to make her see he was prepared to give her coin for the housework she was doing for him, as it was only fair, yet she'd shaken her head.

"I'm in your debt already. You're providing a roof over my head, and I share your bed. In spite of what you may think of me, I would never take coin for being someone's woman."

It had been on the tip of Tom's tongue to tell her he'd paid Sarah Webb for the housework she'd done for him, even if they'd been lovers, yet Sarah Webb had never resided under his roof and he'd never dreamt of calling her his woman. He fell silent under Beth's steady gaze, understanding he would be offending her if he talked of money between them again. He'd come to perceive she was a stubborn woman – in the days he'd gotten to know her – just as determined and as set in her ways as he was. And, in spite of what she'd done in the Square, he'd soon come to see she was no thief. He thought upon the look of sheer misery and despair he'd glimpsed upon her face that day, and upon the malicious, predatory smirk on Sir Lambert's face. He could see very well how a man like Sir Lambert could ruin the life of a woman with no family left to protect her. And he thought of himself, understanding he was perhaps not much better than Sir Lambert, since he'd made a woman in need into his mistress. Still, that didn't change the fact that this woman had a stubborn mind of her own and heeded him only when it suited her. Because this was how Beth behaved – she did all things her own way, he'd already come to see.

After their dazed rapture over the new member of their household, Micah, Declan and William had already started grumbling because Beth had soon taken it into her head to improve their lives in ways she thought fit. She'd started scolding them over their lack of cleanliness or slovenly habits, about bad manners or coarse language. And this did not endear her to the boys.

"I swear," Declan complained mournfully. "She might look like an angel, but I'm beginning to think she's a true fiend sent now on this earth to torment us."

He had just been on the receiving end of a tongue lashing from Beth for his unkempt appearance. Micah and William muttered their ready assent.

"Well, you did spank her in the Square, Master Tom," Micah ventured timidly. "Perchance if you spank her again…"

A pointed look from Tom stilled the boy's tongue, although all three apprentices had started looking at him expectantly. When Tom made no answer and returned upon the hinges he'd been fashioning, Declan, as always the boldest among the boys, ventured to talk again.

"She is a sharp-tongued woman. Don't you think a good spanking might make her sweet-tempered?"

Tom cast Declan an even more pointed look than the one he'd given Micah, which caused the lad to hastily return to his work. Tom shook his head, smiling within himself. Beth was sharp-tongued indeed, they'd all soon learnt, and liked to vent her displeasure. Yet she also often laughed and joked with the boys, and meant well when she scolded them. And while he fully intended to spank his woman if need ever arose again, it was not for her sharp tongue he would ever spank her. This was not something that troubled him in the least. As always, he was content with his hard work which took up most of his time, and having someone who'd taken his household in hand was a thing that pleased, rather than annoyed, him. Beth had begun concerning herself with the boys and was attempting to provide lessons he couldn't teach them as well as she could. So Beth's sharp tongue suited him fine.

"So far Master Tom hasn't been on the receiving end of Beth's sharp tongue." He heard Declan mutter behind him. "But wait and see, soon she will try to rule over him just as she now rules upon us."

Tom was certain the lad had meant for him to hear his words, but, before he could turn to rebuke him, Declan wisely made himself scarce, since it was already near lunchtime.

At lunch, Tom had occasion to see that Beth's sharp tongue had indeed done its work because the boys' table manners seemed far more guarded than they used to be. They no longer slurped down their meals, nor did they wipe their mouths with their sleeves. It was a thing he would not otherwise have noticed, as he was usually engrossed in thoughts of his work, yet the boys' complaints and Beth's talkative presence had made him more mindful of such things than he'd been in the past years since he'd parted from his wife.

At present, he became aware that, as was their habit, his

apprentices were squabbling over their meal. He suppressed a deep sigh knowing how well they loved to quarrel. In truth, he'd long resigned himself that all his meals would be spent in the sound of the boys' arguing. Unusually, Declan was silent at this time, as the squabble was taking place between Micah and William.

"If I'd ever counted how many times you called me a dimwit... And if it's three hundred and sixty-five days, just as Master Tom says... Twelve times a day... For three whole years... Reckon how much that amounts to?" William was complaining.

It was, of course, an endless, pointless quarrel the boys had been having forever, and no one really expected an answer to the question.

"Thirteen thousand one hundred and forty," Beth answered in an absent-minded fashion as she'd begun to clear away their bowls.

"That's right!" William beamed, then started frowning upon Beth. "Truly?"

"Truly," Beth answered with an unconcerned shrug, as she was taking the bowls away to scrub.

All three boys looked to Tom for confirmation, because none of them was strong with far simpler reckonings, and it took Tom a while to figure out the numbers in his head. Yet, in the end, he came to understand Beth had had the right of it. Three hundred and sixty-five multiplied by thirty-six was indeed no more and no less than what she'd said.

"She has the right of it," he conceded, as he took a sip of his ale.

"No? Really?" William asked incredulously.

This led to the boys giving more numbers to Beth to work on in order to prove she hadn't tricked them, as she was busying herself scrubbing their bowls. Her answers came fast and were rather absent-minded. Each time the boys looked to him to confirm whether she had the right of it. Tom could deal with the numbers, but every time he needed a while to think upon them, and, when the boys began to make the numbers even harder to put together, Tom understood he would need an abacus to figure them out.

"Just leave me be!" Beth told the boys tiredly at last. "I told you there is no trick I'm using. I can just do the numbers in my head and that's the end of it."

"I always thought women could not reckon numbers even half as good as men," Micah muttered in the astounded silence that followed.

The others nodded their assent, and yet again looked to Tom to back them up. Tom finished his ale in one gulp, then rose from the table.

"Yet by now it should be already plain to you that some women can do so far better than some men," he said with a smile, knowing he had to go back to his hammer and anvil.

He returned to his work with a shake of his head and a lingering smile on his lips. Fancy that! Beth's astounding speed for reckoning numbers... In the last days he'd perceived she was quite clever, but it was not until today that he'd realized how clever she was indeed.

BETH CURSED under her breath when she finished cleaning up, knowing too well she shouldn't have revealed her uncanny ability with numbers to Tom or the boys. Only her family had known and used her skill, and they'd always advised her to be careful not to display it to strangers. Her mother had feared people would start whispering and call her a witch for her uncanny gift, while her father had been more concerned over her making a good match.

"Most men do not like it when their women are cleverer than

them. So it's best to show just some of your cleverness and not all of it," he'd advised.

Beth had known her father had meant well, yet his words had strangely hurt. And both her parents' advice had robbed her of some of the pleasure with which she reckoned numbers in her head. But now she'd forgotten herself, and had gotten caught up in the boys' silly game. She'd perceived they'd grown to resent her in the last days. And now she expected they'd resent her even more. Whereas Tom… It was hard to tell what Tom actually thought because he wasn't a talkative man. But she reckoned he might not be pleased that his woman was better with numbers than he was.

But when it was time to seek their bed, Tom did not seem changed towards her. He loved her more slowly and tenderly than he had other times, and Beth found herself liking his sweetness just as much as she liked his usual passionate fierceness. Still, when they were done and Tom was lying beside her in bed, with a small smile of contentment on his face, she couldn't help but fret over what had gone on earlier. Tom had not said anything about her gift. Did this mean he already resented it? It was enough that the boys already seemed to hate her…

"So what did Micah, William and Declan further say?" she blurted out, rather artlessly.

Tom adjusted his pillow.

"Of what?"

"You know!" she said perhaps too forcefully.

"Of your sharp tongue?" Tom inquired with a yawn.

"No. What? I'm not sharp-tongued!" she scoffed.

It was true she was forthright, but sharp-tongued? Never!

"Fine. As you say," Tom said in a voice that showed he was already drifting into sleep.

But Beth felt she couldn't sleep. She sat up, discontent.

"I'm not sharp-tongued!" she repeated to herself, hurt that

Tom would think to berate her for an imagined fault rather than praise her for her accomplishments.

"And why would Micah, William and Declan, and why would *you* for that matter take into your heads that I'm sharp-tongued? Because I've told them to mind their manners? And I suppose they're entitled to go on about me, but no one will call *them* sharp-tongued?"

She was now speaking in a high voice, and Tom opened one of the eyes he'd closed.

"Desist! I wish to sleep in peace."

Beth didn't pay him in any mind.

"Just because I will no longer stand for them making a pigsty of this place? Oh, the unfairness of it!"

Tom sat up.

"Right," he said tersely.

Beth was uncertain how a man as large as he was could move so fast at times. Yet she had to own up he was uncommonly fast whenever he took it into his head to put her over his knee, Beth mused, as she found herself lying facedown over his lap.

"Will you desist now?" he inquired, giving her bottom a light, yet nevertheless stinging slap.

"No. I am sharp-tongued! Remember?" Beth countered venomously, although she belatedly recalled her bare bottom was at this very moment at his mercy.

Another slap landed on her bottom, slightly harder than the first.

"Never fear. I've found a good cure for your sharp tongue," she heard Tom say smugly, and she huffed, trying to wriggle out of his grip.

The movement didn't help, because he was holding her fast. So all she did was manage to rub her body against Tom's bare cock. The cock in question promptly stirred.

"This time I am not going to tend to that, Tom Reed!" she told him attempting to give her voice a dignified note. "And," she added pointedly, "I swear I'll scream murder if you swat me again!"

"Aha," Tom said and he didn't seem duly impressed by her threat. "And who's going to pay any mind to you? Do you think Micah, Declan and William will leap to your defence? For a while now they've been begging me to warm your behind."

"What?"

"Come to think of it, it's not such an unworthy thought," Tom mused with a sigh, but to Beth's surprise, he allowed her to wriggle off of his lap.

Beth rubbed her bottom with a dark glare at him. She had occasion to see he was struggling to keep a straight face.

"So fine of you to laugh. You're not the one with a bruised bottom!"

"I barely touched you," he countered with a downright smirk.

"Barely? That from a blacksmith? With a hammer of a hand?"

Tom instantly frowned looking upon his large hand.

"I spanked you far harder before, and you didn't complain even half as much!"

"Oh, but that was before," Beth countered with a snigger.

"Before what?"

"Before you called me sharp-tongued!"

She fluffed her pillow, and presented him with her back. A silence followed, and Beth thought Tom would settle into sleep. She scoffed when she suddenly felt him press against her from behind, although she found her quim gushing as soon as she felt his cock prodding against her bottom.

"I said I wasn't going to tend to that," she muttered, yet to her own ears her voice sounded unconvincing.

Tom began to plant tantalizing kisses upon the back of her neck, while his hand slid to cup her breast, beginning to toy with her nipple.

"Desist! I wish to sleep in peace!" she said pettily, mimicking his earlier words.

She didn't truly expect him to comply, but to her surprise, Tom rolled away from her with a sigh.

"That's all you have to say?" Beth couldn't help asking.

"I didn't say anything," Tom countered, yet he rolled back, and turned her on her side to face him.

He proceeded to rain sound kisses upon her face, breasts and shoulders, and soon Beth forgot to be angry with him, and could hardly keep from smiling. Her smile vanished though when she heard him say in an utterly wicked tone of voice, "I promised not to lie to you. So I must say I think you are sharp-tongued."

She opened her mouth, yet she didn't have a chance to speak.

"Sharp-tongued, but diligent, and very, very, very clever," Tom told her between kisses.

Beth nearly preened under the praise, because, in truth, he hadn't ever praised her before. She couldn't hold her peace though, "Are you trying to sweet-talk me?"

"Indeed I am," Tom spoke against her lips. "Though it is true you're diligent and clever."

They didn't speak again until they were both lying sated after the lusty lovemaking that they shared.

"Do you think they'll grow to hate me?" Beth asked with a sigh.

"Who?"

"You know, the boys. They..."

"They're just a tad upset you seek to change their ways. It will pass. Besides, they had occasion to see you are quite clever."

"But that won't help. They'll only resent me more!"

"Nay. Why would that be?"

"Because... Oh, you know it as well as I. In men cleverness is thought a virtue. In women... a sin. Just like a sharp tongue!"

"I see. So that's what's been troubling you."

She nodded, and Tom put one arm around her.

"Don't let it trouble you. I do not mind your sharp tongue. And I am not as petty as to want to sneer upon your clever mind.

I see it as a gift, not as a flaw. And so will certain other people. Those who are fair and do not feed on envy."

Beth thought she'd melt under the warmth of the embrace. And she savoured its deliciousness, burying her head into Tom's shoulder and not wanting to think of anything right now other than being with him. It was belatedly that she heard him speak, and realized she hadn't been paying any mind to what he'd been saying.

"What say you?" he asked.

"About what?"

"You've not be listening to me, woman," he said, giving her ear a nuzzle and her bare bottom a playful swat.

"Forgive me. I wasn't. So what was it you said?"

"I had been saying that it seems a shame for you to do just household chores when you're so good with numbers."

"I do not mind the household chores," Beth said in earnest. "I have been happy to do them."

And it was so. Once she'd put to rights the things that had been long neglected, the housework here had become light – and she'd always liked to keep busy. Besides, the three growing boys reminded her very much of the brothers she'd lost. Even if they resented her scolding them, she felt it had become her duty to take good care of them, just as she'd always done with her younger brothers.

Tom waved his hand.

"The boys will have to help more with the housework. They were the ones to deal with it before you came."

Beth harrumphed.

"And a fine job of it they did. Dust and cobwebs all around."

"Fine. If you're content doing all the housework, then I'll hold my peace," Tom said in a placating voice, and stirred her thoughts away from the talk.

Sometime later, when they had finally had their fill of love-making for this night, Beth found her voice to ask Tom, "But what did you mean before? When you said the boys could help with the housework? Did you mean for me to help you with your ledgers?"

He chuckled.

"I've had to get used to how clever you truly are. If you were able to read and write, I'd ask for your help with the ledgers, yet what I had in mind was you teaching the boys more of numbers and them showing you how to write them down as well as the letters."

Beth sat up with a frown.

"But I can already read and write. Both Norman and English. Not Latin though."

Tom shook his head in wonder, then cast her a smile.

"It's well then that you can already. Not many women of our station can, and, for that matter, not many men. I taught myself, and I taught the boys some. But I'm no good with numbers and the ledgers are something I loathe."

Beth beamed. At home, she'd always been the one to keep their ledgers, and in truth the only one of her family to read and write well.

"So would you be ready to trust me with the ledgers? Even if not six weeks ago I tried to steal from you?"

It still chafed to think she'd been ready to let go of her honesty, but things were what they were. Yet Tom cast her a steady glance.

"You're not deceitful. And I came to understand you were grieving over your kin's death. What you did was reckless, but people who are grieving are bound to do reckless things."

He said nothing further, just taking her hand in his, and she was grateful for the warmth of his touch, and also grateful he'd brought himself to trust her.

"It would be no hardship to keep the ledgers for you if you wish. Just as it would be no hardship to keep doing all the housework."

He stared at her, and muttered something under his breath.

"What?" Beth asked impatiently.

"But it would be unfair to ask so much of you," he told her in earnest.

And Beth recalled that day when Tom Reed had given her his hard-earned money without asking for anything in return. She hadn't even brought herself to thank him for the deed. But she knew too well that only a man like Tom Reed would do a thing like this. She'd watched him, even when he wasn't paying any mind to her. At first, it had seemed all he cared for was his work at the Forge. But she had watched him with his apprentices. And it was plain he was fair and caring to them. Too soft on them at times, in truth, even when he tried to be fierce. Always soft hearted even if he didn't want to let it show. And seeking to aid others in whatever way he could, rather than try to take advantage of them.

"Nay. Not unfair. I'd like to help," she said brushing a kiss on his lips.

Tom shook his head and cast her a steady glance.

"I will think upon a way. A way which wouldn't burden you with more chores."

He shushed her with a kiss of his own, and settled her head upon his chest. Later, when they were drifting into sleep, Beth vainly tried to tell herself she wasn't already losing her heart to Tom Reed.

CHAPTER 6

William, Micah and Declan grumbled when Tom told them they would have to do some of the household chores they'd happily let fall on Beth's shoulders, so she could help with the ledgers. But he lightened their workload at the Forge by taking more upon himself now that he had more time, and the ledgers would not be falling entirely upon him.

At first, Beth protested she could manage all she'd done and the ledgers, but he warned her it would be unwise to argue, casting her a pointed look, which made the boys grin and elbow themselves and whisper that, finally, the master would give Beth the good spanking she deserved for nagging upon them. Beth glared at them all, but had to comply with what had been settled. And in the weeks that came, Tom had occasion to see his choice had been even wiser than he'd thought. Beth's eye was sharp, and instantly caught the mistakes he'd made adding numbers up, because he'd always been with his head only upon his blacksmith's work and not on figures. And as she took things over, coin, which had always seemed scarce in their household, appeared to be more plentiful. She always recalled which customer owed what, and soon started to deal with customers in his shop, aided by his apprentices. This left Tom more time to spend at his Forge, and, as such, he could not be happier, because seeing to his work in peace was the only thing he craved in this life.

It was upon a morning that Beth called Tom into the shop, to tell him that a lord required his patronage for a contraption little seen before in their land.

"What does he want?" Tom said, rather morosely, because he didn't like to deal with customers and had soon become quite used to Beth dealing with them when they came to his shop.

"He said he'll speak only to you of it," Beth told him. "Besides, he doesn't seem to like dealing with a woman. You know fancy lords are like that."

Tom nodded with a sigh, heading to meet the fancy lord in his shop. Beth soon left him to deal with his customer, going to the house where she'd left William tending to their fare for the day.

"Your woman?" the lord inquired with raised eyebrows staring after Beth had left, with his mouth pursed in displeasure.

"A woman who works for me, my lord," Tom said, knowing it would be always best to hide how things truly were with Beth from people such as this lord.

"A woman keeping ledgers?" the lord asked with an arched eyebrow.

Tom didn't answer, yet the lord kept staring after Beth.

"Her ways are bold. Too bold," he muttered in displeasure.

"How may I be of assistance?" Tom asked tersely.

The lord dismissed his servant, who looked fearful when the lord glanced upon him, and Tom didn't like it that this nobleman had sought his shop. He now already feared he was a nobleman of Sir Lambert's sort.

"I wonder, Master Smith, if you could make this for me?" the lord inquired, placing down a piece of parchment with charcoal sketches on it. "It is a contraption I've long thought of. And I believe you'll see it is quite clever."

In spite of himself, Tom's eyes lit with interest. He always liked to learn of new things, and it was upon a rare occasion that any of his customers brought any kind of drawings with them.

The first drawing depicted some kind of mask. But, when he looked better upon it, it seemed to him both a bridle and a muzzle. He shook his head in sheer wonder. The second drawing his customer showed him was that of a woman wearing this mask upon her face and mouth. Tom stared at it, feeling blood rise in his temples. He'd heard of such things – vile ways of silencing others for punishment, but he'd never seen one.

Mistaking his reaction for delight, the customer preened, "How do you like my punishment for a sharp-tongued wife? See how..."

"My lord, I am not that kind of smith," Tom cut him off tersely. "So you will need to take your business elsewhere."

The lord frowned in puzzlement.

"Yet I've been told you are an able smith and always eager to try to fashion new contraptions."

"They must have also told you I've never made torture implements. That's not my craft."

"Torture? Fair punishment I'd say for shrewish women. Do you know how my woman presumes to speak to me? Master Smith, if you did, you'd hurry to do my bidding!" the lord said with a grim set of his mouth.

"As I said, you will need to take your business elsewhere," Tom countered firmly.

The uneasiness of what he'd seen lingered with him, and when Beth came to ask him whether he'd taken the commission from the lord who'd come, he spoke rather sharply to her, without revealing the reason for his displeasure. Beth looked at him askance, but didn't press, yet Tom's bad mood lingered during the day. Somehow, he couldn't remove the picture from his head, the servant's fear, and the lord's grim, determined smile when he'd spoken of punishing his sharp-tongued wife.

And come their evening meal, he had occasion to hear the word, that was now troubling him, muttered by Declan when Beth was engaged in one of her usual lectures to the boys.

"Sharp-tongued shrew," Declan muttered, as Beth was clearing away the table.

"What did you say?" Tom found himself uttering in a loud voice.

The look on his face must have been menacing, because Declan suddenly no longer looked like his impudent self, but rather white in the face.

"Instead of berating others, you'd do well to earn your keep and clear this table," Tom added making his voice calm, but stern.

Declan gaped at him, and Beth shrugged, coming to the boy's defence, although the lad didn't deserve it in the least.

"No need. I'm used to doing it."

Tom shook his head.

"Nay. Declan should do it from now on. And he should learn to mind his own sharp tongue."

In the rather stunned silence that followed, Declan was forced to comply. Tom watched him with grim satisfaction, knowing it was time for the boy to learn to mind his manners around the woman who tended to their house and business. He then thought of how upset Beth had been when he himself had called her sharp-tongued. At the time he'd just laughed about it and hadn't understood why Beth would find it so upsetting, but now that he recalled the lord's strange, twisted drawing, he was beginning to understand why. And he recalled how Beth had flinched when Sir Lambert had called her a harlot, and promised himself to always keep her from ever coming to harm from such men.

~

As she was putting on her shift for the night, Beth finally decided to ask Tom why his mood had been so foul this day, hoping his bad humour had already well passed. Tom sighed.

"Never you mind," he muttered.

"Never I mind? But I do mind," Beth retorted, because she'd had enough of his sour mood today.

It was after a while that she finally coaxed Tom to tell her of the lord's twisted contraption. A chill went through her spine, as she pictured it.

"May the Lord have mercy on this man's poor wife!" she said, with a sad shake of her head.

Tom nodded with a concerned look upon his face, and she pressed herself against him, understanding she was dangerously close to losing her heart to this man who could not bear it when he thought of others suffering or being treated unjustly.

"Is that why you punished me yourself in the Square?" she asked, because they'd never brought themselves to speak of this. "Because you already knew the guards' punishment would be far more dire?"

He evaded her question, saying instead, "But you did deserve a punishment!"

She let him be, because she understood he didn't like it when others saw how soft his heart truly was. Instead, she mused more upon the lord who had come today, thinking of him and of Sir Lambert, and of how the noblemen of her acquaintance seemed far more unkind than common folk.

"Fancy lords are so cruel! Do you know the story of the lord who had his wife wear a chastity belt on her nether parts while he went to the Holy Land? The poor woman died from it – and no wonder. To be compelled to wear that thing upon your body and be forced to endure filth and discomfort and neglect!"

Tom cocked an eyebrow.

"You do not believe that tall tale, do you?"

"Tall tale? But aren't noble husbands always threatening their wives with making them wear chastity belts?"

"Aye, but have you ever seen one? A true chastity belt?"

Beth frowned.

"Of course not. Where would I have seen one? I do not live among lords or ladies!"

"I have not seen one either. Or heard of such contraptions ever coming to be. And I'm a smith. I know my trade. Do you not think I'd have heard of it if it were true?"

She creased her brows.

"You're saying the chastity belt is all a lie? A tall tale to scare wives with?"

"Most likely," Tom nodded.

"Hmm." Beth wasn't entirely certain he had the truth of it. "But, as a smith, do you think one could be made?"

He burst out laughing.

"Why? Would you like me to make you one? So you can withhold the key from me whenever I want to lick your pretty quim?"

Beth had already learnt not to blush when Tom spoke boldly of what they did during lovemaking. Instead, she'd found she liked this kind of talk.

"Wait," Tom went on, with dark eyes dancing full of mischief, "perhaps you want me to take the measurements for one right now!"

Without giving her time to argue, he went down, parting her legs and making a show of inspecting her quim. Beth was already beginning to blush, but she soon forgot her embarrassment when Tom's clever tongue found her already wet opening.

"You wait!" she couldn't resist saying breathlessly. "What

does your tongue have to do with measurements, Master Smith?"

Yet soon she could speak no more, as Tom's practiced tongue began to work its craft, making her melt with rapture.

CHAPTER 7

The next morning Tom had business to attend to, at his Guild, and as soon as she took care of her more pressing chores, Beth decided to walk to the Market, because it was a beautiful day. It was the first day in weeks she'd felt like doing so, and she understood she was finally feeling more secure in her new life, which had proved far better than she'd thought. And she also understood her life in Tom's household had helped her get over some of the grief over her family's loss. Certainly, she still thought of the ones she'd lost, every day, yet her new life now allowed her to think upon fond memories of them, rather than only of the sadness of having lost them.

"Where are you going?" Declan came to say, as she was readying to step into the lane.

"I'll take a walk to the Market," she told the boy, now narrowing her eyes at him, because she'd gotten tired of his wicked tongue.

"You shouldn't. Master Tom said…"

She raised her eyebrows at him.

"Don't tell me Tom Reed ordered you to keep me locked inside the house!"

"Nay, but he said we need to keep an eye on you, lest that lord who fancies you should prowl around."

Beth sighed, because she knew Declan had the right of it, but she was sick and tired of living in fear of Sir Lambert.

"I want to go walking by myself, and Sir Lambert be damned," she said with a shrug, and started walking ahead without minding Declan who'd begun calling after her.

The day was bright, and she pretended not to mind the curious, avid looks the people in the neighbourhood started casting her way. She knew some of these people from Mass and she assumed they all already gossiped that she was Tom Reed's leman, although the story meant for everyone's ears was that she was only his serving woman.

The walk to the Market was pleasant, and she felt cheerful she was having a much-needed outing on her own, although she didn't spend a long time there, knowing there were sundry things to do waiting for her at home. On her way back, as she suddenly looked up, her eyes fell on Sir Lambert's hateful person in front of her.

"What then, did you not think I have my people watching upon your goings?" he asked as he boldly approached her.

Beth straightened her shoulders, knowing there were passers-by about, but remembering he was a nobleman and always thought he could do as he pleased. She started walking faster, without saying a word to him, but he followed.

"Just tell me… Why would you rather be a commoner's harlot? You could have had me instead. I would have showered you with gifts."

She knew it was best not to answer him. So she pretended she hadn't heard him. Yet he caught up with her and barred her path. It was broad daylight and there were people passing by, yet she felt a jolt of panic going through her, recalling how he'd once attempted to force himself on her and she'd barely escaped. He took rough hold of her shoulder, and she slapped his hand away, but he grinned.

"One day I'll have you," he hissed, but then looked around because he knew there were people already glancing at them askance.

He might be a nobleman, but, still, it was broad daylight, and Beth went forcefully past him.

"Why is it that you're chasing me? Just because I'm one of the few women who told you nay?" she called in full disdain, before walking away from him.

When she turned her head she knew he was still following, with a smug, sickening grin on his face. But soon she had occasion to see the grin wiped off his face, as an egg landed smack in the middle of his forehead. More eggs soon followed, simply raining on him, and by the look of sheer horror and disgust on Sir Lambert's face, Beth perceived they were rotten eggs and she could not contain her mirth. Sir Lambert started shouting, cursing and clamouring for the guards, beginning to screech it was unthinkable a nobleman could be attacked in broad daylight. Yet, Sir Lambert's assailants remained unseen, even when two guards belatedly came and half-heartedly began to look for them.

Sir Lambert was still wiping rotten egg off his face, cursing foully, and Beth couldn't help turning her head to call at him, in a voice of feigned sweetness, "Well met, my lord, setting eyes upon you has never seemed more pleasant!"

Sir Lambert scoffed, but could not accuse her of open disrespect for a lord. The dark look he cast her told her he was not done pursuing her with a vengeance. Nevertheless that day hadn't come yet, and Beth got home, with a shake of her head and a broad smile on her face. It was when she finally reached Tom's home and got inside the courtyard that she thought to call for her unseen guardian angels.

"Declan! Micah! William!"

She called rather long and hard for them, and at last, the three boys made themselves seen wearing smirks of pride on their faces.

"Pelting a nobleman with rotten eggs! That was reckless of you!" Beth chided.

"What would you have us do?" Micah scoffed. "Master Tom told us to watch out for you!"

"Aye," Declan agreed. "And you're the one who recklessly went prancing around. We just followed. It would have been your own fault if we'd gotten into trouble."

Beth sighed, now beginning to fear Tom would get angry with her for being so reckless. She'd nearly endangered the boys through her recklessness. Yet she couldn't help but feel elated when she recalled Sir Lambert's stunned look of outrage when the first egg had landed upon him.

"Thank you for watching out for me, truly," she said giving the boys a bright smile.

William and Micah beamed, while Declan gave her a half-grin.

"We stick out for our own, you know," he finally said. "You're one of Master Tom's strays after all, aren't you?"

"Strays?" she asked, not understanding.

"You were a thief in the square when he found you, weren't you?" Micah said.

"I–"

Beth sighed, but then conceded.

"I guess I was."

"Well, I was a beggar," Declan said softly, looking away from her. "Master Tom found me in the gutter and took me with him, to make me his apprentice. And Micah ran away from his former master, and found shelter here. And William…"

William shook his head, and just shrugged.

"No one but Master Tom and William himself know

William's story. And neither one nor the other have ever spoken a word of it," Declan said with a sigh.

Beth looked at the boys, and felt like starting to laugh and cry at the same time. Their stories came as no wonder though. She'd already learned what kind of man Tom Reed was.

"Don't tell him about today… I will. It was my own fault," she said with a sigh.

"Suit yourself," Declan tossed impudently, then he stuck his tongue out at Micah. "My aim is so much better than yours!"

"Oh, it's so not!" Micah bristled.

"Wait, what about mine?" William ventured.

When Tom came home, she didn't tarry to speak herself of what had occurred, because she felt quite guilty for having endangered the boys. If the guards or Sir Lambert had been able to spot them, they'd have certainly gotten the pillory or even a flogging in the Square. Tom listened to her with a frown on his face.

"No harm was done, but things could have been different. And I'm to blame," she said with her eyes downcast, not thinking it unfair at all if he would decide to spank her as harshly as he had that first day they'd met.

For a while Tom said nothing, then he heaved a heartfelt sigh.

"Not truly to blame, you can't even go walking in broad daylight without that fiend chasing after you. *He* is to blame."

She stared at Tom in astonishment. It was not how she saw things, and she'd thought he'd be angry with her:

"But I was reckless! I didn't heed Declan's warning. I knew the fiend was prowling about, and yet I…"

"You've spent weeks nearly not venturing outside. And, truth be told, I can understand why you would wish to walk by yourself for once instead of hearing Declan's prattle."

She widened her eyes at him. She had in truth expected him to shout at her and decide to punish her, yet instead he put his arm around her shoulders.

"Now you know better. You've clearly learnt a lesson. It's plain the fiend's paid someone who watches your comings and goings."

He paused, shaking his head with a grim look upon his face.

"I wish I could find a way to make him stop!"

Beth was still staring at him, and suddenly what had gone during the day became too much to bear. She'd expected Tom to be angry with her, she'd waited for this anger, thinking it was only fair punishment for what she'd done. Yet Tom wasn't angry with her. Although he should have been. She had been reckless. And she recalled the sickening feeling in the pit of her stomach that she'd had when Sir Lambert had touched her. And she recalled that night, in the deserted lane, when she'd had a narrow escape from him.

Tom was now glancing at her with a concerned look on his face.

"How fare you, *dearling*?" he suddenly asked, brushing his big, rough hand across her cheek. Beth understood in astonishment that her eyes had filled with tears, and she felt ashamed of herself, yet now she'd started crying, although she was never so easily given to tears. Tom held her, and she was grateful for the warmth of his embrace.

"It is foolish of me to behave thus. I was not truly frightened, and he barely even touched me. It was not like..." she muttered after a while, reluctant to look in Tom's eyes after she'd made a fool of herself over this.

"Not like what?" Tom asked with a searching glance.

Beth shrugged, loath to tell him of the night when she'd been barely able to fend off a drunken Sir Lambert set on ravishing her in a deserted lane. She'd been in luck he was drunk and not very steady on his feet, yet it had been a narrow escape and she'd known it.

"Never you mind," she said, wiping her tears with the back of her sleeve.

"But I do mind. He already tried to ravish you, didn't he?" Tom said with a dark look in his eyes and bitter twist of his mouth.

"Aye, but he didn't succeed! Nor will he get to touch me again! I will take better care," Beth vowed.

She felt suddenly ill at ease that Tom was still holding her tight, and she disentangled herself from his embrace.

"I'm off to do my chores. No use thinking upon that worthless fiend," she proclaimed, trying to make light of it.

Tom said nothing, but Beth saw that his eyes were still very dark and his face sombre. He went to mind his own work, yet he was tight-lipped and tense all day, and Beth was sorry to have caused him to worry over her.

CHAPTER 8

Tom had spent a sleepless night, but in the morning his head was clear and he'd already resolved what to do. At dawn, he rose and dressed with more care than usual, putting on his Sunday garb. He left before Beth could wake, because he'd promised to be always truthful to her, and he hadn't wanted to lie to her when she asked where he was going. She would have tried to stop him if she'd known.

He went in search of Sir Lambert, knowing the lord might not even want to glance upon him and thinking about finding a place where the fiend would be forced to face him. He knew from Tristram de Brunne, the lord who often came to look upon the swords he was making, that every day the lords and knights convened on the practice field by the Palace.

Tom hoped to find not only Sir Lambert, but also Tristram de Brunne there. Most fancy lords were cruel, yet whenever Tom talked to Lord Tristram de Brunne, it seemed to him this lord was different. Tristram de Brunne was the best swordsman at King Henry's court, and loved swords above all else. This was how Tom and he had met, as Lord De Brunne had commissioned a sword from him, and had liked it very much. From then on, Lord Tristram had started coming to see Tom and inquire about the swords Tom was fashioning. At times, they even tried the swords together, and Tom was grateful for the sword practice with a knight who was more skilled than he was. And he was proud to say he could hold his own pretty well against a knight, even if it was plain Lord Tristram had more skill with a sword than an untrained blacksmith could possess.

The guards barred his way just as he'd expected, because no one but lords and knights and their soldiers were allowed to step on the practice field by the Palace.

"I am Tom Reed, the smith. I've come to speak to Lord De Brunne about a sword," Tom said, pointing to the sword he had fastened at his hip.

At last, one of the soldiers in the guard went to let Lord De Brunne know that a smith sought to speak to him. It seemed luck had smiled upon Tom, because perhaps a quarter of an hour later, Tristram de Brunne came to meet Tom himself with a rather puzzled look upon his handsome face:

"A sword, Tom? Did we speak of it and I forgot?"

Tom shook his head.

"My lord, it is not this. I thought perchance you may help. I need to speak to Sir Lambert and I think he may be on the practice field where lords and knights convene."

Tristram de Brunne looked grim at the mention of Sir Lambert's name.

"He is indeed," he said in a clipped voice. "Why would you wish to speak to him?"

"We've an unsettled matter between us. And I thought that perchance, if other lords and knights were present, he would be forced to listen to what I have to say," Tom spoke, not wishing to hide anything from De Brunne.

Lord Tristram gave him a searching glance, and his countenance seemed to brighten.

"Well, then, if it is an unsettled matter, I'd better help you settle it."

He beckoned the guards to let Tom through, and they headed to that place, which Tom had never set eyes upon, but where everyone knew lords and knights and their soldiers tried their best weapons and liked to practice. Tom soon spotted Sir Lambert, standing aside in a small group of lords and knights who seemed to be doing nothing but chatting and watching the others work hard on the practice field.

"Bertran!" Lord Tristram called, and soon a lord about Tom's own height and build, came to join them in his helmet and hauberk.

"This is my friend, Bertran FitzRolf. And this is Tom Reed – the gifted smith I have been telling you about. The one who makes wondrous swords," Sir Tristram said, and Sir Bertran nodded in Tom's direction.

Tom greeted the lord with an incline of his head, and then Sir Tristram pointed to where Sir Lambert was.

"Shall we go to speak to Sir Lambert then?" he called to Tom.

"Why would you wish to ever speak to someone such as that one?" Sir Bertran suddenly said to his friend, and his voice was filled with disdain.

"Tom has something to settle with him. And I want to hear this," Tristram de Brunne countered.

Sir Bertran glanced from Tom to his friend, then at last he nodded, and they headed to where Sir Lambert was. Sir Lambert looked uneasy when at last he glanced upon Tom. He tried to pretend Tom wasn't even there and he strived to make him appear beneath his notice, yet Tristram de Brunne called to him in a cheerful voice.

"You know Tom Reed, the smith, don't you, Sir Lambert?"

"Nay, I don't believe we are acquainted. I don't make it my habit to consort with peasants," Sir Lambert countered and the lords surrounding him tittered.

Tom cared little for their opinion of him, and stared Sir Lambert straight in the face, yet Sir Lambert wouldn't meet his eyes.

"Strange though," Sir Tristram said in the same cheerful, melodious voice. "That sword you carry upon your hip which everyone admires. Isn't that your own craftsmanship, Master Reed?" he added, turning to Tom.

"It certainly is, my lord," Tom said, still staring straight at Sir Lambert.

It was the sword Tom had first made for Sir Lambert, before he'd known of his character. And it was upon liking this first sword that Sir Lambert had commissioned a second, the second sword he'd never gotten to wear.

Sir Lambert looked rather green in the face, but he attempted to laugh the whole thing away.

"Oh, I forgot. One smith looks so much like the other."

The lords around him tittered again, but neither Lord De Brunne, nor his big, broad-shouldered friend seemed to share in these lords' mirth.

"My lord, I came to speak to you upon a grievous matter," Tom said, using Norman.

Several of the lords around Sir Lambert raised their eyebrows to hear a commoner speak flawless Norman. And they fell silent, eager to listen.

"There is a woman in my household," Tom started.

"Oh, isn't it always about a woman." Sir Lambert laughed, causing the others to share his merriment.

Yet again, neither Sir Tristram nor Sir Bertran joined in the mirth.

"You should let the man speak and say what he has to say," Bertran suddenly said in a level, yet steely voice, and Tom saw at once that the lords around Sir Lambert had fallen silent.

Tom knew he needed to seize his chance.

"You're not to glance upon her again. You're not to touch her again. *Ever again,*" he uttered in a calm, yet loud voice, which reverberated on the practice field.

Several heads turned, and Tom knew too well that they all understood he was a commoner who'd spoken presumptuously to a lord. Yet there was no turning back from this. In the deep silence that followed, Sir Lambert decided to speak with a disdainful sneer.

"You dare to speak to me this way? And you presume to think I'd have any interest in your whore?"

Tom looked him straight in the eye when he uttered the word. And Tom's face must have looked menacing, because he felt Tristram's placating hand upon his shoulder.

"I'll fight you. Here and now," Tom tossed out to Sir Lambert loud and clear for everyone to hear.

Again, deep silence fell, and Tom knew too well, as a commoner, he didn't have the right to issue a challenge to a lord. But he also knew other lords and knights were watching, and Sir Lambert would look a coward if he refused an open challenge on this practice field, even if it was a mere commoner who had uttered it.

Yet Sir Lambert was a coward indeed.

"I won't dirty my hands to fight with a commoner. Besides, commoners are not even allowed to touch knightly swords," he said in a disdainful voice.

Some of the lords around him acquiesced, yet others fell silent, now watching Tom intently.

"However he is a smith, and he is most certainly allowed to touch swords. There's a fine sword of his own making hanging on his hip right now," Sir Tristram said in his melodious voice.

"As if I'd ever let my own sword clash with a sword that's not knightly. As if I'd ever let myself be touched by a hand that's not that of a knight!" Sir Lambert said rather hastily.

Deep silence fell again, and Tom nearly cursed under his

breath. He'd not expected even Sir Lambert to be so cowardly. Yet it seemed Sir Lambert was more so than he'd thought.

"Oh, fine," Sir Tristram said at last with a heartfelt sigh.

He peeled away the leather gloves he was wearing and handed them to Tom.

"He shall wear these. These are the gloves of a knight, so you, Sir Lambert, need not fear a commoner's hand may ever touch you. And he shall use my own sword. A knight's sword," he added, unfastening the sword he wore from his hip.

Tom saw it was the very sword Sir Lambert had wished for and that he'd ended up selling to Lord Tristram.

Sir Lambert looked even more uneasy, yet he tried his luck one last time.

"What of hauberk and helmet?" he tossed. "The peasant carries none and I will only fight in the proper manner. Where would he find these?" he added pointedly.

Tom had never fought as knights did, in a hauberk, and now Sir Lambert was triumphantly glancing at Sir Tristram, because Sir Tristram was slighter of form than Tom, and this lord's own hauberk may not fit him.

"I'll let him borrow mine. We're about the same height and build," Bertran FitzRolf said at once, and Tom saw Sir Lambert pale.

Yet it seemed now the lords around him were in favour of watching a spectacle, because they'd started urging Sir Lambert to teach the presumptuous commoner a well-deserved lesson.

"No one will mind if you end up slashing his throat," one wispy lord called in a disdainful voice. "He's just a commoner. You'll only have to pay blood money for the killing, and I daresay it would be blood money well spent."

A crowd of lords and knights had now gathered, and some laughed at the lord's joke, yet some looked grim and silent. Sir Bertran and Sir Tristram called for their squires to help Bertran out of the hauberk and Tom into it.

"It's somewhat different to fight in one than without it," Tristram de Brunne advised, because, having fought Tom, he obviously knew Tom wasn't used to fighting in armour. "Your movements will be slower. It's quite heavy!"

Tom nodded. He'd never fashioned a hauberk, because swords and not armour was what he liked to make, but he was well used to handling metal. Metal had spoken to him ever since he was a child – a gift that ran in their family, his father had always said. So he resolved to treat the hauberk as he would any other thing he fashioned and strive to hear that strange inner voice which told him what to do. Perchance he'd hear it when he handled the hauberk.

"Thing is," Bertran FitzRolf added, "you are a big man, just as I am. Use this to your advantage. The hauberk's heavy. It will slow you down. Yet you've got strength. Tristram here relies on skill and speed in a swordfight. I have some skill as well, yet not as much speed. Strength's what I have. I reckon you have that too."

Tom nodded, grateful for the advice. The hauberk leant heavy on him when he went to meet his opponent, yet his heart seemed light in his chest. He had a job to do, and he'd resolved to do it. Sir Lambert would learn today never to lay a finger on Beth ever again.

So the swordfight started, and Tom had occasion to see Sir Lambert was not unskilled, and he was faster on his feet than Tom was in the hauberk, because of long years of training in it. Yet, Sir Lambert was still a coward, and he fought like a coward, always pulling back at the slightest sign of danger. Tom soon came to perceive, if he fought like mad, throwing his caution to the wind, and kept ceaselessly attacking, Sir Lambert's parries became ever so weak. Tom was a big man and, just as Lord Bertran had advised, he used his big bulk to his advantage, moving forward and pushing, rather than pulling back or ducking. Tom didn't know how much time passed, because he became frenzied during the fight, but at long last he saw with satisfaction that he'd managed to knock Sir Lambert to the ground, and when Sir Lambert tried to rise, he didn't tarry to lay the tip of his sword on the fallen knight's neck. And as he did so, he bent to speak softly, yet several of the knights and lords around them had occasion to hear what he said in English, which he knew most lords here perfectly understood.

"Next time you dare to follow or touch her, a sword just as sharp as this one will finish the job it started today. And I will not care if they hang me for it after that. I will have your blood... my lord."

He added the title as an afterthought, putting all the disdain he felt for Sir Lambert in it. He then drew away, handing the sword to Lord Tristram with a gracious incline of his head. There was a longer silence which followed, and after the squires helped Tom out of Lord Bertran's armour, several lords started casting Tom dark glances. Still, most of them gazed at him in a way which, Tom began to see, looked very much like grudging respect.

One of them even called out, "He fights quite well, for a commoner, that one. Pity he isn't noble-born."

Tom had never wished himself to be noble-born, yet he felt good under the praise. And he felt even better, when both Sir Tristram and Sir Bertran patted him on the back.

"Well done," Bertran FitzRolf said with a broad grin. He soon added with a sigh, "You have humiliated him, and you should have a care. Sir Lambert is most spiteful."

"I know a lady though," Tristram de Brunne mused. "A lady we can put to good use."

Both Tom and Bertran frowned at him, yet Tristram enlightened them with a smile.

"This lady is friends with Sir Lambert's wife, and Sir Lambert's wife is of high rank and from a family more powerful than his. Should she know her husband is so avidly chasing another woman, and acting like a fool, she would be none too pleased."

"Trust My Lord Tristram to know a cunning way out of this," FitzRolf said with a grin and a shake of his head.

"But Bertran's right. You have humiliated Sir Lambert, so have a care," Tristram advised.

Tom made his thanks to both lords for their gracious help, thinking he'd been right indeed to seek Sir Tristram out, and understanding, upon having also met Lord FitzRolf, that not all noblemen were of Sir Lambert's ilk. He headed home, back to his Forge, with a self-satisfied grin on his face, and he kept that grin all day. Fortunately, Beth seemed too busy with her own chores to ask him where he'd been this morning, so he did not have to share the truth with her.

She only told him with a frown, not having missed his grin of self-satisfaction, "Why, Tom Reed, you look mightily smug today!"

Tom only shrugged, pretending to be too busy with his work to answer.

CHAPTER 9

The next day was hot, and Tom found it unusually hard to work in the sweltering heat of the Forge. So he decided to take some respite, and went to the kitchen to drink a cup of ale, because he had become quite thirsty.

He found the kitchen even hotter than the Forge on this scorching day and he eagerly poured himself the cup of ale he'd been craving. Beth, who'd been busying herself with their meal in the kitchen, now arched an eyebrow at him.

"You're all sooty from the Forge! And this is a kitchen I've been taking great pains to keep clean!"

Tom drank his ale thirstily, but nodded at what she'd said when he was finished. It was true, she had been working hard in both the house and with the ledgers, and it would not do to disparage her work. He noted the dark smudges he'd already left on the table he'd leant on.

"I'll take more care in the future," he promised with an incline of his head, yet already beginning to think back upon the iron plough he'd been fashioning.

It was always like that when he was in the middle of his

work. He became preoccupied and frenzied, and somewhat unmindful of those around him.

"See that you do!" Beth's sharp voice roused him, and she was glancing at him with narrowed eyes.

It was a hot day, and she'd been working hard. Even with his head upon his own work, he couldn't fail but notice the way her gown had become plastered upon her ample bosom. At present, Beth carried a wooden spoon in her hand that she no doubt meant to use to stir the pot which was merrily boiling on the stove.

A mischievous thought sprang into Tom's head.

"Oh," he said, making his voice surly on purpose. "And what are you going to do next time, whack me with that wooden spoon, if I don't have a care?"

"You think I wouldn't dare?" Beth countered, bristling at him, but Tom noted at once her own voice carried teasing in it.

"Would you?" he countered, cocking a dark eyebrow at her.

"For sure, Master Blacksmith, even if you think yourself so big and strong and mighty!"

Tom instantly decided his work could wait a while, because, as always, he was ahead with it. He closed the distance between them in two long strides, and took possession of the spoon Beth had been holding. He liked the feel and weight of it in his hand. And he found himself already savouring what he was going to do with it. It was somewhat strange that, before he'd met Beth and had put her over his knee, he'd never been concerned with this kind of strange love play. Yet he instantly resolved that it was Beth's own fault, for having such a naughty, well-rounded behind that always seemed to beg for chastisement.

"Yet I *am* bigger and stronger than you. And now the spoon is in my hand," he muttered, already lowering the spoon to give Beth a light whack over her clad bottom.

She glared at him, but Tom could see, at the same time, she could barely contain a smile.

"It's so unfair! You're the one who came traipsing all over the kitchen!" she made a show of complaining.

"Aye, this world's most unfair," Tom said with a deep sigh, as he was leading her to the table.

Beth looked at him in some alarm. "What are you doing?"

He bent her over the table, hoisting her skirts.

"Proving to you how unfair this world is," he said suppressing a chuckle.

Her ample bottom was just as scrumptious as he recalled it to be since this morning when he'd been caressing it, while he'd been embedded within her sweet quim to the hilt.

"Wait? Wh-what?" Beth asked and there was some alarm in her voice.

He didn't give her time to finish, but whacked her with the wooden spoon across her bare skin. The whack was mild and would not sting much, yet it was enough to already leave a delicious pink mark on one of Beth's pristine buttocks.

"Think upon this as a reminder that *you* should always behave," he said wickedly, bestowing yet another light, playful whack upon her behind.

"So unfair!" Beth muttered, yet he noted with a supressed smile that the protest in her voice was accompanied by a half moan.

He used the spoon a couple of more times, a bit harder, yet not hard enough to cause any real discomfort. What he was going for was a mild sting that would make his woman wild for his thrust. Because as soon as he made sure she was wet and moaning, he intended to thrust inside her for quick, delicious loving. He discarded the spoon, replacing it with his hand, because he was now dying to feel her skin heating beneath his palm. He bestowed light, teasing spanks upon her bottom, savouring both its silky warmth and the pinkness that soon appeared there. He paused his spanking, putting his fingers to work upon Beth's quim, which was already wet.

"I trust you've learnt the lesson I meant to teach," he said teasingly, as he was tending to her.

"What lesson?" his sharp-tongued woman immediately countered. "More like unfair punishment!"

Yet she was already breathless with want and had already started thrusting her naughty behind at him.

He gifted her with a hard, stinging smack, then grabbed her hips, positioning himself for entry.

"Wh-what?" Beth muttered. "Like this?"

Tom smiled to himself, recalling, so far, he'd never had her from behind. He adjusted her position to his liking, choosing not to answer her question. Soon she would get to see for herself the full benefits of this new way of loving which he meant to show her.

"Ahh," Beth moaned, in sudden understanding, as he slid his cock inside her slick quim.

"You were saying?" Tom couldn't help asking in full mischief, as he started driving in and out of her, loving the deeper way in which he could possess her from behind.

He was very aroused, and soon he understood it would be best to withdraw and pause in order to prolong her pleasure. So he withdrew from her body, gritting his teeth, aware of her deep sigh of regret.

"Tom," his woman purred, and he knew only too well what she wanted.

Yet he would give her even better than that. He spanked her lightly, still having her bent across the table. Soon her bottom became more heated and almost red under his spanks, and she nearly peaked, moaning wantonly.

It was then he entered her again in one fluid thrust, driving hard inside her and loving the warmth of her freshly spanked bottom as it made contact with his front. Even when he knew she'd already climaxed, he drove in and out of her with a vengeance until he found his own release, knowing with certainty he'd never loved being inside a woman as much as he loved being inside this one.

It took a while for both of them to collect themselves, and it was belatedly that Beth ran to the pot which smelt burnt. And Tom supposed that, if they'd not been so wrapped up in their naughty lovemaking, they would have both been able to perceive the smell.

"Oh! Look what you've made me do! The potage is as good as ruined!" Beth cried in full chagrin.

Tom grinned with an unconcerned shrug, because for all he cared she could now feed him pig slop. He was far too content at this time to mind what he'd eat tonight.

Beth scowled at him darkly.

"You're a fine one to smile, Tom Reed, when I'm the one who has to see to today's meal!"

Tom decided they would all treat themselves with a meal from the cookshop, and resolved to send William to fetch it. Yet, by the way Beth had menacingly taken hold of the wooden spoon, he thought it more prudent to tell her of it a bit later and to make himself scarce at this time. Nevertheless he couldn't help adding some mischief.

"I forgive you for the ruined meal and I vow not to spank you for it!" he called loftily as he was hurrying out of the kitchen.

He paused outside to listen, with a smile, to the things Beth was calling after him from the kitchen, thinking she was now giving him the perfect excuse to spank her again and nearly resolving to go back to do so. Yet he had work to do, and she had her own chores, so he headed back to his anvil with a sigh of regret. He hadn't had the courage to tell her that the back of her gown and parts of her own delicious and somewhat reddened skin were now smudged with black, because she'd after all been the recipient of tender ministrations from a master blacksmith. By the dangerous heights to which her voice now rose, he understood, with a renewed sigh and a shake of his head, that she'd been at last able to perceive the damage for herself.

At the Forge, the boys started casting him strange glances when he resumed his work, and he belatedly realized he wore a wide smirk upon his face which must make him look stupid. He tried to wipe it, but simply failed.

Declan cleared his throat.

"Ha, Master Tom, I don't really see what you're smiling about. I think the whole neighbourhood could hear her giving you the sharp end of her tongue."

"Aye, even my ears blushed at some of the things she shouted," Micah chimed in.

As usual, William was silent, yet he shyly nodded in assent.

Tom shrugged, attempting to cast them a stern look and tell them to mind their own business. Yet he was unable to look stern at this moment. He supposed he was still wearing a silly grin of contentment upon his face.

"Back to work, lads," he muttered, not knowing what else to say, and blissfully recalling to send William to fetch a meal for them from the cookshop.

After a while, he realized he'd even started whistling to himself as he worked, a thing he hadn't done in long years. And he realized there was another thing he hadn't felt in years that he was experiencing now. He was... happy. He hadn't felt genuinely happy in a long while, and he understood it was the woman who had so suddenly come into his life that was making him so. At first, he tried to chide himself for feeling the way he did. Yet he could not. It was only ten weeks since Beth had first entered his home, yet now he simply could not picture how grim and joyless his life had been before he'd met her.

~

BETH PRETENDED to be angry with Tom for the rest of the day, yet she was, in truth, beginning to see their life had settled into a course she had not envisaged. Certainly, there was deep lust between them, and her quim became wet whenever she thought of the delicious way he'd had her from behind and of the playful spanking she'd received. Yet, she had already perceived they were behaving towards one another more and more like man and wife. Tom had become able to guess most of her moods, and already knew the things she would enjoy and those which would tease her. He was mischievous and warm in truth, and that temper he professed to have was mostly sunny rather than fierce. He always threatened to take her over his knee for a harsh lesson if she misbehaved, yet the spankings she'd received ever since she'd entered his house, even the sterner one he'd delivered on the night after they'd first bedded, had been more teasing and playful rather than harsh. He seemed to have guessed only too well what kind of spanking she was ready to handle without resenting him.

Today when he'd left the kitchen with that smug, self-satisfied grin upon his face after their lovemaking, she'd nearly forgotten he was not her true husband. Yet he never seemed to forget they were not wed, and always took care not to spill his seed inside her. And he was not her husband, which meant she might never get to bear his children one day. At first, this hadn't mattered, but now it did, because Beth understood only too well she could now no longer envisage a life for herself without Tom Reed in it.

She felt restless all day, and, when Declan had a moment of respite, she couldn't help herself and went to sit by his side, to ask him those questions that had, for a while, been on her lips. She was loath to ask Tom those questions, but maybe Declan would help answer some of them.

"What of the wife?" she asked abruptly, and Declan frowned

at her, yet it was plain he understood only too well what wife she was talking about.

At first, she thought Declan wouldn't want to tell her, but the boy raked a hand through his red hair and sighed.

"He never speaks of her, so you'd better not ask. It pains him still."

Beth widened her eyes.

"What did she do?"

To her, it seemed plain that Tom was not the one to blame for the failure of his marriage. She could find no fault with Tom, whatsoever, although not in a hundred years would she ever admit to him she liked each and every thing he did in this world.

"You're never to tell him I told you! She…"

Declan paused, then winced before speaking.

"She lay with his brother."

Beth opened her mouth, stunned.

"What?"

Declan nodded, with a shrug.

"What did Tom do?" Beth asked with widened eyes.

"What do you think he could do?" Declan said, shaking his head bitterly.

Beth knew that punishments were dire for such offenses and she recalled the way Tom had shielded her from her own dire punishment from the guards. She reasoned Tom had been faced with two courses, that of denouncing his wife to the Church, or that of punishing her himself. She already knew Tom would have spared any woman from a gruesome punishment, and, even if he had taken the punishment into his own hands, he would have also felt compelled to give a measure of forgiveness to the miscreant. Yet Tom's wife wasn't here, which meant there'd been no punishment and no reconciliation.

"They parted ways. And where is she? A convent? But he'd be free to marry if she'd truly taken the veil..."

"She now lives with his brother," Declan answered tersely.

Beth shook her head in wonder, but then couldn't help but sigh. The first time they'd met, Tom had let her have his hard-earned money even if she'd tried to steal it from him. Because this was how Tom was. Kind and giving. So instead of ruining the life of both his wife and his brother, he'd let them have their own happiness, at the expense of his own.

"They're far away from here, I assume," Beth muttered.

"I reckon," Declan shrugged. "They left in the dead of the night with Master Tom's blessing. He claims not to know their whereabouts, but I think he has an inkling where they are."

Beth nodded. Of course, Tom would protect them to the end, although it was plain they'd hurt him deeply.

"What was she like?" she asked, before she could call back the words.

Declan smiled faintly, with a shake of his head.

"Not as sharp-tongued as you are, if that's what you wish to know. Yet not soft-spoken either. Nevertheless, not at all as you are. Not always strangely cheerful. Sad."

"*Sad*? He'd done something to make her sad, you reckon?" Yet Beth shook her head the moment she'd spoken the words. Tom was not a man to make a woman suffer. He was mischievous rather than harsh, and even when he felt he needed to be harsh, he was not unkind.

"They made each other sad, I'd say," Declan muttered with a shrug, rising to go back to his chores.

For the rest of the day, Beth mused upon what had been said, yet, when night came, she did not ask Tom about any of it, although there were many curious questions lingering in her head. She resolved Tom would speak to her of them in his own time. For now she was at ease she was not the one to be keeping him from his lawful wife. And she understood there could be no reconciliation ever between Tom and his former woman. So Beth resolved to consider herself Tom's woman in every way from now on. She would not ever part from him unless he asked it. She loved him – and it was not a thing upon which she thought with shame. Rather, she thought upon it with a strange, secret joy. Yet it was a joy mixed with concern and care for the pain Tom had been through.

That night she was very sweet to him, and he ended up loving her quite gently. Yet he frowned upon her when they were done, when she attempted to lay her head upon his chest.

"Something amiss?" he asked, perusing her intently.

"No. Nothing. All is well," Beth replied because it was indeed true she felt content with the way things had turned out in her life.

He propped himself on one elbow to look at her.

"You're not scolding me or driving me out of my mind with your prattle. And, unusually, you're not doing everything in your power to make me lose my patience… not misbehaving in any way."

She laughed.

"What? Do you wish me to?"

He cast her an assessing look, but then he smiled rather ruefully.

"No. Not at this time," he said after a while, now embracing her and settling her head on his chest.

And as she fell asleep, Beth began to think that happiness was perchance not that hard to find. But in the next days she had occasion to see that hard to find it may not be, yet it was awfully hard to preserve.

CHAPTER 10

Tom began his morning with good cheer, yet soon he had cause to see his good humour vanish entirely. It was when talking to an old customer regarding a price for a pair of knives that he had cause to hear Beth clear her throat behind him.

"A word I pray," she said, and, as Tom turned to her, his customer gave a slight, mocking laugh.

"Already keeping you upon a string, I see," he said, casting a knowing smile at Beth.

Tom did not like how the man presumed to speak of what he saw in front of him. Yet things were what they were, and he was well aware that all and sundry knew Beth was his woman now. Glancing upon Beth, he had occasion to see her face was suddenly set and determined.

"In fact, I meant to remind Master Reed of the new price he set for knives. He used to charge ten pence, but now it is a shilling."

Several pairs of eyes fell upon Tom because all three apprentices were standing by, and had been able to hear the exchange.

And Tom became painfully aware of the look of flustered puzzlement which had certainly appeared upon his face. He saw his customer's mocking eyes and knew at once what the man must be thinking. Master Tom Reed was now letting his woman rule over him. He conjured up the tale the man would tell everyone who would wish to hear. Tom Reed was forever doomed to be scorned by his women. His first had run off with another. And his second had already made herself his mistress in everything.

"My serving woman is mistaken," Tom found himself saying stiltedly. "It's still ten pence for knives."

He fought hard to contain his dark anger when at last his customer took his leave. And he strived to keep his distance from Beth because he knew he was enraged with her. Yet the confounded woman wouldn't let him be.

"Wait!" Beth called, striding after Tom into the kitchen. "The boys have told me this man has been long taking advantage of your generosity! He's well to do and can afford to pay a fair price. Besides, I did not like the way he looked upon us."

Tom's jaw tightened.

"I do not like to be belittled in front of my apprentices. Nor my customers," he told her with a frown.

Beth waved her hand.

"It was not what I meant, and you well know it."

"Perchance. But that doesn't change things. You overrode my word in front of all to see," he said grimly.

"I did not! I merely said we talked upon it. And you must see it's better to…"

"Better? Clearly, you knowing better how to conduct my trade than I do!"

Beth heaved a sigh.

"You do not like to keep the ledgers. And you do not care to concern yourself with coin. For the past weeks I've been doing it in your stead. So why feel belittled when I do the work you entrusted me with?"

"This is just glib talk, and we both know it. You overrode my word."

In spite of what he may think of her, Beth had never been a liar. Not even when she'd nearly turned into a thief.

"Fine. Aye. I overrode your word. Will it make you feel better to chastise me for it?" she said wearily.

There was a silence before he answered, and Beth found she would have preferred his anger to the bitterness with which he spoke.

"No," he said tersely, and then fell coldly silent as he was pouring himself a cup of ale.

Beth told herself she should feel content he was not the sort of man who felt he should chastise her whenever they did not find themselves in agreement. Yet she didn't. In truth, she'd gladly have taken a chastisement instead of his cold contempt.

"Fine," she retorted. "But I'll have you know, again, I do not think what you charge is fair. It's way too little!"

When he didn't answer in return, just staring at her with a look of grim displeasure, she went on impassionedly, "That is not what my father would have charged in Winchester. And this is London! Prices are steeper in London!"

He frowned at her.

"It seems to me now you think yourself entitled to rule over my business," he tossed at her in a bitter voice.

"Aye, since it's become plain to me you have no wish to rule it," she countered.

He said nothing, just staring at her with pursed lips and clenched fists. She shrugged, because she'd never been a woman to mince words, and she had vowed to be always truthful to him.

"You work like mad, yet you gather next to nothing from

your hard labour. Not for yourself and not for the boys who are apprenticed to you. You live from hand to mouth, although you are by far the best smith in London and toil harder than any man I know."

"Work is its own reward. I care for my work," he countered with a set look upon his face.

"I know you do. And so you should. Yet, have you thought of that day when you're no longer able to work? What will happen then? When you're old, or ill, or injured and you find you've not saved anything to rely upon in your hour of need? What then? Will you be begging in the streets?"

She wished to tell him more, yet she was loath to share with him her whole sad story, loath to tell him how her prosperous household and their earnings had started to crumble away the year her father and brothers had been taken by the fever. How the priest's malicious lies had forced her and her ailing mother to leave their home and livelihood behind in haste, taking with them next to nothing. How she'd nearly become a thief out of need.

"You need to think of hard times! You know I'm right!" she pleaded instead.

But Tom just cast her a dark, stubborn look.

"Aye. Perhaps it is as you say. I live from hand to mouth, with no thought of tomorrow. It is the way I want it though. You speak of what will happen to me in my old age and you seem to mind. Yet I cannot bring myself to care for what will happen. My home… My trade… What good are they when there's no true family? When I know there'll never be sons or daughters who can inherit what I've worked hard to achieve? When my craft and the work I do is truly all I have to look forward to?"

The words were spoken in an angry tone, seething with bitterness. And Beth felt her heart clench for him. Yet Tom was wrong to think himself so unfortunate. Couldn't he see, while he may never have any children, the boys he'd apprenticed already loved him fiercely as if they were his own flesh and blood? And couldn't he see, no matter how he felt, he already had her heart? That he would always have her heart?

She opened her mouth to speak, but she was taken aback by the sheer fury in the next words he uttered. She'd never seen him so angry, not even that day in the Square, and she nearly recoiled in fear from the pitch-blackness that became his eyes.

"Stop looking at me like that, woman! Stop looking at me with pity in your eyes! I will not bear your pity! And I need none of your meddling!"

He stomped away angrily, without sparing her another glance, and Beth was left to stare after him. She heaved a sigh, already having come to know Tom Reed and being well aware his temper may flare at times, but that he was ultimately a man able to see reason. He was in pain. Yet she felt certain she could make him see his fate was not as grim as he thought it to be. He might not return her love or wish to heed her advice. Yet, in her heart, she already knew he'd grown to care for her in his own way.

TOM WALKED AWAY ANGRILY, feeling a dark mood descend upon him, although his day had started out so well. And he found himself retracing his steps to the place, he realized now, he'd not visited in several weeks. It was the furthest corner of his garden, a little patch where he'd planted a linden tree. No cross marked the grave, though a grave it was still, the grave of his almost son.

And Tom recalled that night of rain and wind, when he'd stood in the birthing chamber, hearing his wife's screams of unspeakable pain and witnessing her terrible suffering, unable to do anything to soothe it. He'd been able only to watch what was being done. At last they'd taken the child out of her in pieces, because no other way was found that could save her.

That night he'd paid the barber surgeon who, not two hours before, he had raced like mad through the city to fetch for his wife. And then he'd paid the midwife who had been unable to save their unborn babe, but who had done all she could to save Joanna's life. Then, while Joanna lay in her exhausted slumber, he'd taken away the remains of the dead babe to bury at the back of the garden. He'd already known too well no priest would bless the grave of an unbaptized child, so he'd said a prayer and had fashioned a blessing of his own to say over it. He'd then gone to sit at Joanna's bedside, fervently wishing for her to live through the night. And Joanna had mercifully lived, yet a piece of her had died that night, and he supposed that, the very same night, a piece of him had also died, although it had taken a long time for him to acknowledge it had been so.

For him it had been nevertheless easier, because he'd always been able to find comfort in his work. And then Declan came to be apprenticed to him, and he soon grew fond of the boy, a thing which, now that he looked back, must have truly pained Joanna, whose suffering in all this had been far greater than his. In the beginning, he'd been unable to understand why Joanna would resent the boy, but by that time, things had already grown strained and silent between him and his wife.

He'd tried at first, in his own way, but perhaps he hadn't known the right way to do it. He'd stayed away from his wife for a long time, loath to share her bed and endanger her life. She had already miscarried twice before she'd borne this third child to full term, but the first two miscarriages had been in the very early days of her pregnancy and she hadn't been harmed or too grieved by them. Yet this third pregnancy had nearly claimed her life, and Tom was not as foolish as not to understand what the midwife had attempted to tell him, when she'd come to look upon her recovering patient.

"It isn't that her womb can't quicken. It's not that her hips are too narrow or that her body isn't hale. Yet I have seen this often.

It might simply be that she'll never be able to bring a live child into this world even if her belly swells and she carries it the full time. Yet you're both young, and God may show mercy upon you. Prayer and pilgrimage are bound to aid you! Have a care though, bedding is to take place only after you've given your woman proper time to heal!"

"But… will she be fully healed? She suffered so much," Tom had muttered, white in the face.

"I cannot tell you such suffering won't happen again if she gets with child. Or that a new childbirth won't claim her life. It's all in God's hands," the midwife had said with a sad shake of her head.

So Tom had refrained from bedding his wife, even long after the time required for healing had passed. And then he had resolved that, no matter the penance the Church might see fit to bestow upon him, when he did, he should not give her his seed. His wife had nearly died along with their child, and he felt loath to endanger her life like that again. Yet even after he'd made this resolve, Joanna had no longer seemed to want him in her bed. One bitter night, she'd plainly told him she thought him fully responsible for what had happened. It had been certainly because of his lustful ways in bed. It was not for naught that the Church decreed that coupling should be restrained. Their loving had been too lustful, and their sin had now been punished by God Above. Tom had in vain tried to reason with his wife, telling her that, if this were really true, then most people on this earth, which included parents and siblings and friends and neighbours, would be all terribly punished for such sins. Yet it had been to no avail, and he had not pressed on, thinking that time would heal Joanna's fresh wound.

For a while, Joanna tried to find her solace in piety, yet at last she gave up on it, because it had never been in her nature to be very devout. Yet when she finally allowed Tom back in her bed, their couplings became joyless. She still wished for a child, even at the cost of her own life, and this caused further strain between the two of them. Soon the couplings stopped altogether, and the talk and laughter and tenderness they'd once shared also simply ceased, as if there was nothing left to say to each other.

It was when Tom's brother, Robin, came back from his travels with his tales of mighty cathedrals and wondrous towns, that Tom finally had occasion to see Joanna smile and laugh again. And he rejoiced in it, thinking that, at last, time had healed her wound. And in a way it had been so. Tom now raked a hand through his hair, remembering the deep rage and grief at the time when he'd found Joanna in his brother's arms. He glanced upon the linden tree he'd planted over his son's grave, recalling how the rage had subsided. Yet the pain over it and over his lost child had lingered, until a woman unlike any other he'd known had suddenly crossed his path.

He retraced his steps to the house and found Beth, who was, as usual, busying herself with a chore. She glanced at him rather warily, and he heaved a deep sigh.

"These past months you've been working hard, with nearly no respite," he started artlessly.

She'd tried to talk reason to him, and he'd shouted at her. The price she'd pointed out had been fair, and he had been in the wrong to ask for less. And then he'd berated her for his own hurt pride.

Beth shrugged, straightening an errant tendril of her hair.

"It's how I want it. Besides, you also work hard. I've not heard you complain. You are fond of your work."

"Aye, and I know you also like to keep busy. But tomorrow's Market Day. I thought we might walk through the Market together and spend a day of leisure looking at sights and wares," he went on, only belatedly recalling that even at Mass they were always careful not to stand next to one another and they'd never even walked together in full view of others, knowing people were already gossiping about them.

"Fine. Yes, gladly," Beth suddenly told him with a warm smile, and he nodded in return with a smile of his own, not having the heart to tell her he'd erred in asking this of her.

CHAPTER 11

Beth frowned, patting her well-worn gown, but then shrugging and deciding not to care what she was wearing. She'd seldom gone out lately, for fear Sir Lambert was still pursuing her. Sir Lambert hadn't been seen in a while, but he was certainly dangerous enough to still want to harm her, and the guards were bound to turn a blind eye to it, just because he was a knight and she a commoner. Beth had learnt her lesson that day when Sir Lambert had pursued her, and had avoided leaving Tom's household ever since, although of late Tom himself had told her to stop worrying at every turn about Sir Lambert. He seemed to believe the lord was no longer a danger, yet Beth was still cautious. And then there was the trouble of Tom accompanying her in full view of others. She already knew tongues were wagging that she was not just a mere serving woman, but was living in sin with the blacksmith. The priest in their church had already chided her for it and given her penance at confession. Yet the penance was light and consisted only of prayer, as the old priest in this parish was fortunately a kind and mild man, different from the churchmen of her own acquaintance. So Beth decided that the well-worn gown, which had seen better days, was the last of her worries now. She had already resolved to go to the Market with the man who now shared her life, and nothing was going to stop her.

Beth strived to put such bleak thoughts aside as she and Tom walked to the Market. And soon the bright day and the joyous hustle and bustle around them made her feel more cheerful and think less of how things truly were. Instead, she pictured Tom and she were married and had just decided to share a day of leisure at the Market. They strolled around for a while looking at the wares, yet Tom soon took her to the cloth merchant's stall.

"Take your time to look at the wares," he told her softly. "And don't fail to purchase what you deem right for gowns and such. Next week we're bound to visit a friend of mine who's a master shoemaker."

She blushed, knowing full well how well-worn her gown and footwear looked, but loath that he should think she would demand him to buy her new things to wear.

"I don't truly need anything," she muttered, because well-worn they might be, her dress and shoes had been bought when her father's household was still prosperous, and they were her best, and still quite sturdy, because she kept them in good repair.

He cocked a dark eyebrow at her.

"Your work with the ledgers and figures of my trade has already brought me good coin I wouldn't have gotten otherwise. Methinks you've already earned the things I urge you to buy."

"But you need to remember that purse of money you gave me that day when you..."

He frowned at her, halting her with a gesture, and telling her softly, "Need I threaten a spanking as harsh as that one to make you cease your protests?"

Beth blushed scarlet, glancing warily around them, hoping no one around had heard their talk. Reluctantly, she inspected the bolts of cloth, deciding to choose a fabric that was cheap yet sturdy for her gown. When she inquired after it, Tom came to stand by her side, and pointed to a bolt of deep green, which was decidedly more expensive, and upon which Beth had earlier looked. She'd looked at it quite longingly, but it was expensive, and she didn't want more expense incurred on her account at this time.

"How much is this one?" he inquired, and didn't even think to bargain when the seller told him the price.

"Nay!" she protested, but Tom shrugged her off.

She glared at him when they left the stall with the bolt of cloth upon which he'd paid an outrageous price.

"I hope you know that merchant robbed you blind!" she told him pointedly.

He shrugged, with an unconcerned smile.

"I do not truly like to haggle," he told her, as if that was the most natural thing in the world.

"I do!" Beth countered.

"Then next time we purchase something *you* should," he said in return.

She narrowed her eyes at him.

"I most certainly will!" she warned him, understanding this was the only time in her life she'd acquired something without haggling.

Still, she glanced lovingly at the bolt of cloth that Tom was now carrying. She couldn't help noting it was fine cloth indeed and acknowledged to herself with a suppressed sigh that the merchant wouldn't have lowered the price by very much even if she'd haggled fiercely.

"Do you think I'll look fine in it once the gown is cut and sewn?" she asked, unable to help preening a little.

Tom shrugged.

"What are you asking me for?"

She raised her eyebrows at him, but he went on, "You shouldn't be asking me. For my part, I think you'd look fine even in sackcloth."

"Sackcloth?" she asked with widened eyes.

He paused, then muttered, somewhat flustered, "What I meant is that you're a fair-looking woman no matter what you choose to wear."

Beth's heart simply started fluttering in her chest, yet she couldn't help teasing him:

"I declare, Tom Reed, this is the first time you have found a kind word to say about my appearance!"

They made several smaller purchases of bread and salt and vegetables, and Beth was satisfied to be able to haggle every time for a price she deemed was fair, while Tom rolled his eyes at her. The next stall that they should visit was that of the fishmonger, because Beth wanted to buy their Friday fare. Tom seemed to linger when she pointed out the stall to him.

"Are you coming?" Beth asked him with a raised eyebrow, unable to understand why he hesitated.

Tom still lingered for a short while as if he was making up his mind, but then he nodded. Beth at last saw he was rather reluctant for them to go visit the fishmonger's stall, and soon had occasion to see why that was. The women who were tending it, the fishmonger's wife and her sister-in-law, were from their own neighbourhood and were among those very women who already looked upon Beth with avid, malicious stares whenever she passed by.

"Good morrow, Master Reed," the women called as soon as their eyes fell on them, and Tom gave a brief greeting in return.

As Beth was looking at what the fishmongers had to offer, Tom became engaged in talk with another neighbour who had just happened by and who wished to speak to him. The two women behind the stall kept chatting between themselves, as

Beth was attempting to see if the haddock looked fresher than the plaice, yet they stared boldly at her from time to time.

"Mighty fine bolt of cloth Master Reed is carrying. Yet the green of it is a better colour for a woman such as yourself rather than for a man such as he is," the younger woman said with a sly look in Beth's direction.

Beth shrugged, choosing not to say anything, because she knew that, whatever she said, they had already judged her. The older woman stared away from Beth disdainfully, then muttered to her sister-in-law, as if Beth were not even there, "I bet I know how she earned that."

"Aye," the other woman replied in a lower voice, but she was now somewhat self-consciously patting her headdress.

"She earned it on her back," the older woman muttered with a sneer.

The words had been spoken softly, yet they were loud enough for Beth to hear. Beth bit into her lip, straightening her spine. She simply pretended not to have listened to what had been said, because she understood if she started a quarrel, she would draw even more attention to herself. Instead, she looked at the fish deciding that instead of buying just haddock or plaice, they should have a bit of both.

When she inquired of each price, the younger woman told her the figures in a disdainful voice, not looking her in the eye. The older woman took over and came to stand right in front of Beth behind her stall. Her younger sister-in-law seemed relieved to let her deal with a customer she obviously didn't relish, and began to busy herself tending to a basket of eel.

"What will it be then, *mistress*?" the older woman asked Beth in her sneering voice.

Yet again, Beth pretended not to hear the deep disdain in her voice.

She uttered loud and clear what she wanted, and listened when the woman added up the sum which she needed to pay.

Tom had at last finished his talk and had come to stand by her. He reached for his purse at once to begin counting out the coin.

"Nay, that's not four pence, it's three," Beth said, unable to stop herself.

She had, in truth, already decided it was not worth the trouble to bargain for a better price here, although she was aware the woman was asking a price which was somewhat higher than what she'd have ordinarily paid for this lot. Yet now the woman had added the numbers up wrong. And Beth knew she had done it on purpose.

Tom now counted out the new figure Beth had uttered.

"Here you go then, mistress," he said handing out the money to the fishmonger.

The woman glared at him.

"I said four pence, Master Reed. That's the fair price added up!"

"Is it?" Tom suddenly asked, and his voice was level, yet there was something steely inside it.

"Aye!" the woman shouted quite loudly.

"So add it up for me, once again. Because I know Beth here, who works for me, never fails to add numbers rightly."

The woman scowled at him, and began to mutter the prices half-heartedly.

"That's three for the lot, right?" Tom said with a raised eyebrow.

"Aye. I must have added wrong," the woman said reluctantly, in a querulous voice, casting Beth a venomous look.

"No harm done then," Tom said with a shrug, but his voice held the same steel as earlier as he handed the woman the coin.

Beth strived to keep silent, because it was wise to let Tom handle this. She didn't truly want to draw attention to herself, but it seemed that now several curious gazes had been drawn by the small squabble at the stall.

"Let's go," Tom said after he'd paid the required price and Beth had placed this new purchase in her basket.

Yet, as they turned to leave, Beth heard malicious laughter from the stall they'd just left behind, and the word which was tossed, loud enough for several people around them to hear.

"Harlot."

The word hurt, yet Beth held her head high, telling herself it was of no matter. It had hurt when both the priest and Sir Lambert had spread lies about her. And it still hurt, although now she'd indeed surrendered her virtue. But when she thought upon herself in Tom's arms, there was no feeling of shame she could conjure up. She nearly smiled to herself. Because it was plain to her why she couldn't feel any shame. She loved Tom and she'd probably been born to love him even before their paths had crossed that day when he'd spanked her in the Square.

"What did you say?" Tom suddenly uttered, turning to face the stall with a fierce glower.

The woman who'd obviously called the word shrugged, muttering something under her breath, as she drew away, pretending to busy herself with her fish. Beth placed a placating hand on Tom's shoulder.

"Tom, let it go."

She was aware that some of the people in the Market were staring at them, and she knew they were muttering or thinking the same ugly word which been uttered.

"I won't have anyone malign this woman!" Tom said in a loud voice which was plainly daring everyone in sight.

Some of those who'd been staring returned to their business reluctantly. Yet others were still casting malicious glances in their direction, and Beth understood Tom was wrong to think he could protect her from their scorn.

"I do not mind," she told him softly, attempting to lead him away. "There are far worse things in this world than being a harlot. Better a harlot than a thief. You saved me when I nearly became a thief. And I came to your bed willingly. So if they wish to call me your harlot, it will mean nothing to me. What lies between us is none of their business."

She tried to smile and make nothing of it, although her cheeks had begun to burn. It was not the word that truly hurt. It was the people's mistrust and scorn. And she understood it would be hard to cast away this brand of scorn. It would perhaps forever cling to her.

"Tom, let's go home," she said, making her smile serene and brilliant.

It hurt, but being with the man she loved made all of it bearable. Tom sighed, finally letting himself be led away. They headed home, and for a while they walked in silence, broken at last by Tom who suddenly said, "I'd wed you if I could. Right here and right now."

The words were spoken in a soft, yet decisive manner, and Beth's heart skipped a beat. The way they'd been spoken left no room for doubt. Tom Reed loved her, and in his heart he'd already acknowledged her as his wife, just as she'd already acknowledged him as her husband. She stopped in her tracks, forcing him to halt as well. When he cast her a questioning glance, she threw her arms around his neck and kissed him ardently, not caring there might be people in the street who knew she was his mistress.

Tom first responded eagerly to the kiss, enwrapping her in his strong, blacksmith arms, but he soon became self-conscious and broke it, casting her a warning look.

"I do not care if they see us," Beth said with a shrug and a smile, tracing the kiss on her lips. "I am so happy!"

Tom frowned.

"Happy I'll never be able to wed you? Happy I've made you into a target for other people's scorn?"

"You didn't make me into anything," Beth countered as they resumed their walk. "I chose this."

Tom shook his head with a sigh.

"You didn't know better. And I, who did know better, am fully to blame for how people now look upon you."

"You flatter yourself, Tom Reed. I knew what I was walking into," she countered, now making her voice both teasing and defiant.

"Oh, did you?" he countered, his voice now fully angered. "Did you truly understand you'd be forever forsaking a home and children of your own?"

"I've already found a home!" she countered.

"You know too well what I mean. Even if we have children, they'll be branded bastards, and by my Guild's laws, they may not even be entitled to a small portion of what I own. And *you* will certainly have nothing once I'm dead. They'll cast you in the streets with nothing!"

"Then I truly hope it will be me who dies before you!" she said with a careless laugh, knowing too well what he was saying, but also acknowledging she would never part from Tom Reed in spite of it all.

He fell darkly silent, refusing to look at her, yet Beth knew his anger was born out of love. Her heart was light when they reached their home, because now she knew for certain she had Tom's love and nothing in this world could ever part them, not even other people's malice. Yet Tom was grim and tight-lipped all day, and he pushed her away at night when she tried to win him over with caresses.

"We'd better talk," he said, raking a hand through his dark hair.

Beth nodded with a sigh.

"My wife…" Tom started, but it seemed he had trouble finding his words.

Beth opened her mouth to set him at ease, yet remembered her promise to Declan. The boy had urged her not to tell his master what he'd shared with her.

"What was she called, your wife?" Beth asked, attempting to set Tom at ease to tell the story that he now wanted to share.

"Joanna," he answered with a rueful smile. "She... We wed young and we'd been promised to one another since an early age. In truth, I do not even recall a time when we'd not been promised. We grew up together and were a good match, knowing each other's likes and dislikes by heart. She was my closest childhood playmate, after my brother Robin. Robin – who is the cleverest man I know in this world. He is a builder and dreams only of mighty cathedrals whose turrets soar as high as Heaven."

As Tom told his tale and spoke his brother's name, he thought of Robin and of that terrible night he'd found his wife in his brother's arms. And he thought of the stricken look filled with grief and guilt on both his wife and his brother's faces.

That night, Tom couldn't even bear to look at Joanna or speak to her. She wanted to plead with Tom and tried to call after them in anguish, when he and his brother went to deal with the business that was unsettled between them. Tom had always been larger and more vicious in fistfights, yet Robin was fast and clever and never easy to beat. That night though Tom came close to killing his own brother, because Robin would not lift a finger to defend himself.

"Fight, damn you!" Tom spat at his brother, staring like mad at the bloodied, grazed knuckles of his fist.

Yet Robin shook his head.

"I'll kill you!" Tom shouted.

Robin looked at him levelly, wiping the blood off his lips and face with a calm gesture.

"Then kill me. Me first and then Joanna," he said in a mocking, bitter voice.

Tom felt like starting to weep. Because his brother's voice held a truth that, for a long time, he'd not wanted to acknowledge. Before his brother had come back to their house, Joanna had been slowly dying, and he'd feared that the grief she carried over their lost child would one day kill her, and, like the time she'd been in agony, he would just stand by, unable to help her in any way.

"What you two did..." he said now conjuring up the searing rage he felt towards both her and Robin.

"I've always loved her, too. And I've loved her far more than you ever can," Robin countered levelly. "I went away right before you wed. I shouldn't have. I should have stayed on and married her instead of you."

Tom cast his brother an astonished look, because Robin had never spoken to him of this. He'd never known. And now he heard Robin plead, in a humbled, anguished voice, "Let me take her away! She'll die here and you know it. There's nothing but grief left for her here."

And Tom had known his brother's words to be true, even though he'd hated him even more fiercely for them. He cast a bitter smile to the woman now standing in front of him, who was staring at him after what he'd told her of that night years ago when he'd allowed his wife and his brother to leave together and make a new life for themselves.

Beth clasped his hand.

"You spoke of a lost child."

"My son, who died in the night when he should have been born."

It felt strangely soothing to utter the words. Perchance this was what had forever severed the ties between Joanna and him. They'd never brought themselves to even speak to one another of their dead babe after that night.

"Grief," Beth muttered. "You spoke of your wife's grief. What of your own?"

Beth was the first who'd ever asked him this. He suddenly smiled at her, because it was due to her that he'd finally been able to overcome the grief which had, for so long, loomed over his life.

"Now, I find I feel it no longer," he told her, cupping her face and claiming her lips for a deep kiss.

CHAPTER 12

That next morning Beth felt emboldened by the things Tom had shared with her. And when he attempted to take her in his arms and love her just as was his habit, right after they roused, she did not let him make himself master of her too soon, choosing to tease him with brash kisses and caresses of her own. She traced the hard muscle of his chest and licked his round arms, and pushed away his strong hands when he wanted to pull her to him.

"Ha! Getting bold now, woman?" Tom Reed said with an arched eyebrow, yet his own voice was laced with teasing.

She did indeed get bold and dared to pin his arms to his sides, so Master Reed, the blacksmith, was now at her mercy.

"Not so high and mighty now, *Master* Smith," she said softly, moving to straddle him and speaking against his lips.

He did not make an effort to release himself from her hold, yet he attempted to capture her lips with his. She didn't let herself be kissed, which made him furrow his brow.

"Too bold, I'd say. Bold women do get their comeuppance, didn't you know?" he threatened, yet he still did not attempt to release himself from her hold.

Beth laughed, beginning to rain teasing kisses on his neck and shoulders.

"Perchance I could talk my way out of the punishment you must certainly have in store for me, Master Smith? Is there any means by which I could atone for my deeds?" she said between kisses.

"I reckon I can think of one," her prisoner muttered, a mischievous sparkle dancing in his dark eyes.

He soon told her what he had in mind, and Beth only belatedly recalled to blush at what he now asked of her. She kissed her way down his taut belly to reach the stiff cock that he wished she'd tend to. Feeling just as brash and bold as before, she smiled against his skin as she lowered her lips to the red tip of his shaft.

"Like so? You need to school me, I have not done this before," she said, making her voice quite innocent and coy.

In truth he had not asked this of her before, but Beth had left behind her maidenly shyness for some weeks now, and she soon found herself revelling in the hard length of her lover's cock against her lips. And she also found herself revelling in the new power she soon discovered she possessed over her lover.

"Oh, it seems that, for once, it was you who lay at my mercy..." she told him at last, when she wiped her mouth and looked upon his sated face with a triumphant smile.

"We shall see about that," her lover vowed in an ardent voice, and, in the next moments strived to prove to her that she could be just as easily brought to his mercy.

There was a taste of Tom still lingering on Beth's lips, when they decided to start their day and she began to hum to herself as she was readying breakfast for the boys who'd just come in the kitchen.

"A beautiful morning," Tom said, gazing outside.

"Aye," Beth readily agreed.

Declan cleared his throat.

"The sky is grey. There's a storm brewing…"

He and Micah and William were casting glances at both of them filled with what seemed like astonishment and pity.

"Both on their way to madness it seems," Declan muttered with a sudden smirk to the others, because he couldn't help using his glib tongue.

"Don't you have chores to do this morning rather than dazzle us with your prattle? Such as helping with breakfast instead of waiting to be served hand and foot?" Tom said, but his tone of rebuke was mild.

The rest of the morning that had begun so well passed uneventfully, yet later that day, while she was busy with her ledgers, Beth heard the sound of voices and went outside to see what was happening. She found Tom and the boys there, along with a small crowd of people who had already gathered. In the centre of it stood none other than Sir Lambert, accompanied by their parish priest. He cast a satisfied smirk when he at last glanced upon her, and with a cold stab in her heart, Beth began to understand that the day which had begun so well held peril for her.

"And here she is, the woman I've been speaking of," Sir Lambert said in his heavily accented English.

TOM FOUGHT HARD NOT to strangle the man in front of him with his bare hands. Yet Sir Lambert was a lord, and Tom knew only too well the odds were against commoners in this battle. A dire punishment was in store for him if he ever harmed a nobleman. And while he might be ready to forsake his life just in order to rid the world of Sir Lambert, he knew his actions would mean peril for those he held dear. Beth and the boys would suffer if Tom were to do something reckless.

"This is the woman who works for me keeping my house and

ledgers. And what of it?" he said in his turn, striving to keep his voice level.

"She is a lewd woman," Sir Lambert called, making sure the word had been heard by all those gathered around.

Father Septimus cast Tom a look of sheer misery. He was a kind, mild man who seldom bestowed heavy penance on any of his parishioners, but Sir Lambert had made an accusation, and Sir Lambert was a lord knight, whose word no one could take so lightly.

"Beth has been summoned to appear in front of the archdeacon in three days hence," Father Septimus said in a reluctant voice, casting a fearful glance in Sir Lambert's direction.

"Summoned?" Tom said, as fear began to seize his heart.

A summons could not be ignored. And, even as a blacksmith well regarded in his own Guild, he did not have the authority to oppose a summons from the Court Christian. Lay people were summoned by the ecclesiastical court only when they stood charged of loose morals. It was upon a rare occasion that an archdeacon or even a parish priest concerned themselves with petty matters such as a married man keeping a mistress, yet it was plain Sir Lambert had made it his business.

"So, Master Blacksmith, perchance now you will get to see the real colours of the woman you've let inside your bed and home," Sir Lambert said, with a satisfied smirk upon his face.

Tom's hands itched to grab the knight by the neck. He glanced at Beth who was staring at both Sir Lambert and the priest, white in the face. He'd never seen her that frightened, not even that day when she'd been accused of thieving in the Square. And he resolved he would protect her no matter the cost.

"Three days hence then," he said in a voice which was calm and unconcerned. "Thank you, Father. And, thank you, *sire*," he added in flawless Norman, stressing the *sire* in such a way that left no doubt his view of Sir Lambert's person.

Sir Lambert cast him a look of sheer venom.

"You will come to thank me, Master Blacksmith. This woman is not who you think she is. It has just of late come to my attention that her soul is even blacker than I thought. Perchance you didn't know she already stands accused of seducing a priest in her hometown?"

Tom strived to receive the words with an unconcerned shrug, and not to glance too much at Beth whose face had gone an even sicklier pale. Yet she was truly distressed, and he felt like putting his arms around her for comfort. It seemed nothing short of a miracle that she even found her voice to speak.

"Three days hence then," she said, echoing Tom's voice, even if her own voice was tremulous. "I shall be there."

She looked only at Father Septimus, not even glancing at Sir Lambert.

Tom strived to think upon what he was to do, with calm in his thoughts. He reasoned peril had come upon them sooner than he'd foreseen. Yet, he had already made up his mind this morning concerning what he and Beth were to do, even before Sir Lambert's presence had darkened his day. He'd thought upon it all night, and had come to the only answer which could be had. He would not have people stare in scorn at the woman he loved. And he would not have her tossed in the streets from her home if something dire ever happened to him. Robin and Joanna had found their own happiness away from London. And he recalled the talk he'd had with Robin on that terrible night.

"No one would know," Robin had pleaded. "We'll pass for man and wife in another town and no one will know. Even if someone is bound to recognize Joanna, I'll lie and say it is in truth a cousin of hers I wed. She looks much changed, paler and thinner than she used to be."

"That would be deceitful," Tom had muttered with a dark frown.

Robin had shrugged.

"Who are we harming? No one will know! And you... You

could sell your business here and start over in another land. A land where you can find a new woman for yourself."

But Tom had shaken his head.

"This is our father's house. And of his father before him. I will not ever leave!"

Robin had sighed.

"At least release us! No one will know Joanna is not my wife!"

Coming back to present times, Tom reasoned he could do the same as his brother had done. He would find a remote place where no one knew Beth was not his wife. He'd already resolved upon this course this morning, and had meant to tell Beth of it this very night. He'd thought he had at least a month to settle things here with his business, yet it seemed time had suddenly grown short. He felt loath to leave with next to nothing, apart from some coin and the clothes on his back, yet he would do so, as soon as he settled the boys with other good masters of his Guild. He would not jeopardize their future by asking any of them to join him. He cared too much for them and would rather part from them because it was best they continue their apprenticeship in London. As for himself, he knew he was a very able smith and would not have trouble finding work. He thought of a remote village where no one would know them and where he and Beth could settle and have a life together.

TOM CALLED UPON BETH, leading her to the house and telling her they needed to talk. Beth glanced at him warily, recalling too well that his face had looked astonished when Sir Lambert had spoken of the priest she'd allegedly led astray. What would he think of her? Beth noted that Tom wasn't asking her anything, but was staring through the window with a set expression on his face. She decided to speak before he even opened his mouth.

"Do you not want to know? If what Sir Lambert said was true?"

"Nay. Because I already know it for a lie," he said quietly.

"So you believe me? In the Square… I tried to steal from you. And now…"

"You did not steal though. And I have come to know you well. You may be many things. Reckless at times. And stubborn. Sharp-tongued at other times. Though not a deceiver. And not seeking to harm others. Never that."

His faith in her made her want to weep.

"Would you like to know what happened?"

"Only if you wish to tell me."

And haltingly Beth told him her tale, recalling how it had been after her father and brothers had died. Her mother had been overtaken with grief, and fallen ill with it, and Beth had attempted to shoulder all the burden of their household, trying to be strong in this time of need. She'd been grateful when the priest of their parish had summoned her, telling her he would speak to her words of comfort. Yet it was a different kind of comfort he'd had in mind.

"He'd not attempted it before!" Beth said with an astonished shake of her head. "He'd always been kind and gracious, comforting, as a priest should be, but now… he propositioned me, boldly."

Tom let out a short, mirthless laugh.

"The fiend. He knew only too well that now you no longer had a father or brothers. He took advantage that you were a woman who'd lost the men of her house."

Beth nodded in chagrin. She had seen, after her father's death, men who hadn't even glanced in her direction had started to look at her with open lust and to whisper behind her back as she passed by. They had begun to speak of her bold ways, although her ways hadn't changed at all since her father's passing. And now Beth understood that while her father and brothers had been alive, those men hadn't dared act. And like them, the priest had now looked upon her as his prey.

"He tried to ravish you. Just as Sir Lambert did," Tom said grimly, perceiving the look in her eyes.

Beth nodded, as he came to put his arms around her.

"Aye. And when I attempted to tell others of what he did, he falsely accused me. They were coming for me at my house meaning to chastise me for what they thought I'd done, and we had to leave our home in haste, taking with us next to nothing of what we had. And then... The rest you know. Here I came upon Sir Lambert."

"Who's still living and breathing, although I should strike him down where he stands," Tom said darkly.

Beth disentangled herself from him. Her heart thumped in deep fear. "Please! Do not attempt anything against him! It will be your doom!"

"And yours too! I know it only too well!" Tom muttered, clenching his fists.

He sighed then, coming to kiss the top of her head.

"We shall leave here. Today, I'll make arrangements for the boys to be re-apprenticed. I hope we can leave this very night or at least tomorrow night!"

She stared at him mouth agape.

"You would leave your house and business? For me?"

He said nothing, just nodding, and again Beth felt like weeping. She had done this to him. He'd been the only man to offer her a helping hand. He'd welcomed her into his home. And now he was paying the price.

"I will not have it," she said quietly.

Tom shook his head.

"There is no other way. They'll punish you. They'll parade you in Church and they'll flog you for a loose woman. And who knows what else they'll do. Much worse..."

Beth nodded in full bitterness, then cast Tom an anguished glance.

"They may bestow heavy penance upon you as well. In their eyes, you're guilty of adultery."

"This is not what I fear! Have you not seen the mad gleam in Sir Lambert's eyes? You now stand accused of seducing a priest! Not only of being my woman!"

Beth weighed all this in her mind, and she thought upon how well-regarded Tom was in his Guild, for being such an able smith, and she also thought that penance was most often bestowed on women for adultery or loose behaviour, and very seldom on men. As long as it was proved she was the one who'd lured him into sin, he would not truly suffer.

"I'll face the accusation. I may be guilty in their eyes of being your woman, but this other thing I am not guilty of. I'll speak my truth," she said, resolve now strengthening her.

As she spoke the words, her heart became light again, and she understood she wanted to face the unjust accusation, only to tell everyone loud and clear that they were in the wrong. And she didn't fear the penance for what she'd done with Tom. She would bear it gladly and take it only upon herself, rejoicing that he, at least, would get to be safe from the Church's wrath. She was the one who'd come into his bed, tempting him, and she would state that for everyone to hear.

He attempted to let her see his anguish.

"You do not understand! You are in peril!"

"Oh, but I do!" she countered, because she truly did, but she would not have the man she loved lose the house and livelihood he had on her account.

Tom now started pleading with her, telling her over and over again what she would face, and pointing out that her very life may be in danger over it, yet she had made up her mind and nothing of what he said could move her now.

"Stubborn, foolish woman!" he shouted at her at last, now at the end of his tether. "You seem to think you have a say in it! But you don't! I'll put you over my knee and spank you hard to teach you to see reason! And then we shall leave this place!"

She shrugged, feeling unconcerned with his threat.

"Then spank me raw, yet I will not relent!"

He glowered at her, his very dark eyes looking fearsome, but she didn't flinch. Instead, she placed a placating hand on his shoulder.

"Tom, I will not run from them. Not anymore."

THE WAY BETH spoke the words was so heart breaking that it simply melted his dark rage over her senseless behaviour. Tom stared at her, seeing the set, grim line of her mouth. And he imagined himself standing by, watching mutely, as she was chastised and tortured in front of him. If they sentenced her, he would be able to do nothing, just as he'd been able to do nothing that night when his wife had lain on the brink of death.

"We'll talk upon this later," he said, now striving to speak calmly.

Beth nodded and she seemed to think she'd won, but she was wrong to think so. Tom had made up his mind, and he would drag her away from here by force if need arose. He would make the arrangements for their departure today. And he would simply hoist her over his shoulder and take her away with him if she still dared to argue.

He was on a hurry out of his courtyard, to go and speak to one of his friends in the Guild, when he bumped into Tristram de Brunne, who often came to look upon the swords he fashioned.

Tom bowed his head.

"My lord, I pray forgive me, I'm in a hurry to do an errand."

Yet De Brunne halted him when he wished to leave.

"I've come upon Sir Lambert today."

Tom nearly winced at the sound of the name. He paused, bracing himself for what De Brunne would tell him. The lord spoke urgently.

"He bragged of how he'd be the downfall of the haughty common woman who'd dared to spurn him. He was already drunk at this time of the day, and bellowed his story to the lords who were eating in the tavern at this time. I happened to be there, and heard it all."

Tom raked a hand through his hair, strengthening his resolve to take Beth away from here as soon as can be.

Sir Tristram went on, in the same urgent voice, "Sir Lambert spoke of a priest in Winchester, that the woman under your roof is accused of seducing. He spoke the name of that priest, Ambrose. Yet, it was a name I knew well, because my own cousin, a woman of high birth and high standing accused him of vile deeds against his parishioners. That priest is now imprisoned and facing trial as we speak."

Tom glanced sharply at De Brunne.

"Did Sir Lambert not know of this?"

De Brunne shook his head, smiling faintly.

"Not many know of this. The Church did not clamour upon what had been done. Besides, I happen to know this from my own uncle who's the Bishop of Winchester."

"A bishop? Henry de Blois?" Tom said, unable to contain his astonishment, because he now understood that the lord in front of him must have royal blood running through his veins.

He glanced at De Brunne, who was unlike most lords he'd met. Sir Tristram was not vain and always listened to commoners when they spoke as if they were his peers. And Sir Tristram seemed willing to aid him again. Yet he recalled what the lord had said of the priest, and he twisted his mouth in a bitter smile, unable to prevent himself from saying, "It is strange, isn't it? No one believed my woman when she accused the priest you speak of. Yet, they believed your noble cousin."

De Brunne gave his own bitter laugh.

"You speak the truth, and it is unfair. It is a very unfair world we live in. One where men like this priest and Sir Lambert get to prey upon women. And it seems unjust that worthy people like you and your woman should suffer because of them. I have resolved to plead with my uncle on your behalf. I hope I shall prevail upon him to come and look upon you."

Tom widened his eyes, in deep astonishment.

"Will such a man even deign to look upon people like us?"

Lord Tristram cast him a steady glance.

"I'll find a way," he said, and his words were assured.

Tom glanced at the lord, understanding God had smiled upon him when he'd set this man into his path. He bowed his head in deep gratitude.

"My lord, I thank..."

De Brunne halted him with a gesture.

"Nay, do not say it. It is my knightly duty to try to right some of the things which are unfair in this world. I just could not stand by."

It was with surprise that Tom took the hand Lord De Brunne was now extending towards him, because never in his life had he clasped hands with a noble lord. His heart was more at ease after he conferred for a while with the lord, and he decided to return to his house, following the lord's advice and wait for word from him.

Beth seemed calm and cheerful after he'd retraced his steps to the house, and he glanced upon her with narrowed eyes and a shake of his head, thinking he should after all spank her for the reckless way she looked upon her own fate.

"You're back already?" she asked calmly, as she was chopping parsley in the kitchen.

"As you can see," he countered grimly.

"I will not leave. So that you know," she suddenly told him in a calm voice, as she busied herself with her task.

Tom's hand itched to spank her right then and there because she was plainly set on endangering her own life, but he resolved there were more pressing matters to take care of at this time.

"We might not need to leave as yet," he said, and he proceeded to tell her what he'd talked upon with Lord De Brunne.

Just as he had, Beth twisted her mouth into a bitter line when she heard the priest finally stood accused of his misdeeds:

"Of course, they would take only a noble woman's word and not the words of all those common women he preyed upon," she whispered.

Tom nodded grimly.

"Things are what they are though, and it is hard to change them. But if we stay, Beth, I want you to listen to me closely!"

She looked at him, and he made himself look stern in order to make her mind him.

"You're to be silent and speak only when spoken to by the bishop. Is that understood?"

She heaved a sigh and looked mutinous, but he glanced at her pointedly.

"I will not have your own recklessness ruin your life!" he said, attempting to make his voice compelling.

"It's not recklessness! They want me silent, just as they silenced me and all those other women when the priest lied! It is unfair!"

He nodded, understanding what she meant, but knowing he had to protect her at any cost.

"Just hold your peace for my sake," he said with a sigh, understanding, at this time, the renewed threat of a spanking would not serve any purpose.

She narrowed her eyes at him, and opened her mouth to speak, yet in the end she reluctantly nodded. Tom suppressed a sigh of sheer relief, promising himself to teach her a much-needed lesson on recklessness when all this was over. Yet he prayed the whole thing would be over soon, and did not feel confident that the outcome would be fully in their favour. While Beth was not guilty of seducing a priest, she was most certainly guilty of lying with a married man. Yet he did not fail but recall *he* was the one who was in truth breaking his wedding vows. And he thought upon how a bishop would see such things, beginning to conjure up in his mind the words he would speak if Lord Tristram's uncle deigned to look upon them.

CHAPTER 13

Beth tried to still her thumping heart as she felt the eyes of the small crowd which had gathered around them. It seemed to her the crowd was as menacing as that day in the Square when Tom had spanked her in order to save her from the more dire fate they'd all awaited. She strived to focus on the present moment, glancing upon Henry de Blois, Lord Tristram de Brunne's uncle, who had deigned to look upon them in a short hour of respite.

The Bishop of Winchester was elderly and frail, and Beth recalled she'd heard it whispered he might not live through the summer, as his health was poor even if his will to live was great. It was also whispered he'd mellowed in his old age and looked upon his flock with more tenderness than before. He was a nobleman, of high birth, and Beth supposed they should be grateful to Lord De Brunne for this great favour. In spite of his ill health, Henry de Blois was willing to listen to what they had to say.

She glanced upon Sir Lambert, who'd also been summoned on the steps of their church to utter the accusation he had against her. The look Sir Lambert was now casting Tom was one of sheer, dark hatred, but Beth understood only too well how cowardly Sir Lambert was. It was upon her he sought to take revenge, thinking her feeble and helpless and unable to defend herself against the unjust accusations. She suppressed a sigh, not feeling reassured by what Tom had told her. The priest may have been found guilty of unseemly deeds, but that did not mean the bishop would look kindly upon her.

"So," Henry de Blois said in a weary voice, "I've little time to spare, yet it seems I must see to this. Sir Lambert, I understand there are words you wanted spoken, and I shall hear them now!"

"This woman brought before you is a harlot, Your Grace. A harlot who lured a priest into sin. A certain Father Ambrose, and now…"

Sir Lambert was speaking in a high, frenzied voice and, suddenly, Beth felt a deep, powerful rage come upon her when he uttered the word he'd also employed in front of Tom. Beth fully recalled her deep rage that day and how she'd stifled it, and how the people in her hometown, her friends and neighbours had been ready to believe Father Ambrose's hateful lies about her. And although Tom had pleaded with her to speak only when spoken to, Beth found she could not hold her peace, though it might be her doom. She would not be silent and hold her eyes downcast.

"Father Ambrose tried to ravish me! A man of God, right in the church, when I was seeking comfort after the death of my father and brothers! Then he lied! And you dare to call me a harlot? You?"

She caught Tom's worried gaze upon her and understood her words had sounded brash and bold and defiant. Beth smiled bitterly to herself in the silence that fell around her. Tom certainly feared for her, yet he could not truly understand the rage burning inside her breast now. She did not fully understand why she burnt to behave so recklessly, although she knew within herself it was wiser to keep silent. Perchance it was blasphemous of her to think so, but she could not stay silent, and cowered, and meek when her life had been nearly ruined.

The bishop frowned upon her and looked thunderous, yet Beth straightened her shoulders, knowing she could not behave otherwise. Lord Tristram de Brunne bent to speak in his uncle's ear, and at last the elderly man looked mollified, waving his hand at her dismissively.

"I'll have no more words from you, woman. You shall be silent! And hear well what I have to say."

Beth found herself wanting to disregard the words, yet she caught Tom's gaze upon her. She now willed herself to be silent, knowing she'd brought this peril not only upon herself but upon him. She did not truly care for the punishment they would wish to bestow upon her, yet she could not bear to have something dire befall the man she'd come to love so dearly. So she held her peace, bowing her head, although her heart ached as she did so.

"It is already known to us the woman is indeed innocent of what Father Ambrose accused her of," the bishop spoke grimly. "And Father Ambrose will be certainly punished for his transgressions. Still, that does not change the fact that Sir Lambert has denounced her as a harlot and that she now cavorts with a married man."

Tom's heart thumped with dread because, in spite of Tristram's assurances, he feared the punishment the Church may bestow upon his woman. So he also decided to speak out of turn, not caring for the bishop's frown of displeasure:

"My lord, I swear upon the Holy Cross the woman came to my bed a maiden, and she did not know I was wed when I asked her to share my bed. May God strike me down right now if I do not speak the truth!" he said fiercely, not caring for the astonished mutters of the onlookers.

The bishop narrowed his eyes.

"You know you're risking eternal damnation if you're lying!"

"I speak the truth," Tom said, now finding Beth's wide eyes.

She opened her mouth to speak, yet he held her gaze, hoping she would heed him this time. Sir Lambert looked from one to the other in sheer malice, yet Tristram de Brunne chose to voice his thoughts.

"What I do not know is how an esteemed lord knight such as Sir Lambert can swear this woman is a harlot. Unless he sampled her charms, but I can't fathom how this can be. Sir Lambert is a pious knight, who's wed. Are we then to believe a knight, such as he is, has sinned against his holy vows?"

There were snickers from the crowd, and even jests regarding Sir Lambert's lack of virtue, which the bishop chose to steel his ears against. Instead he cast Sir Lambert a pointed look. The lord knight squirmed.

"I-I only sought to warn the good people here against this woman. I thought her a harlot, who had lured a priest. Certainly, I have no true way of knowing how virtuous she is."

The bishop raised a halting hand.

"Enough of this. I find my patience has thinned. Sir Lambert, I pray you do not trouble the Church again with petty matters such as blacksmiths and their lemans."

Tom felt too elated by Sir Lambert's long face to take any offence at the bishop looking down upon what he was.

"Sir Lambert," the bishop spoke now and his voice held a strange mixture of silk and steel. "Perchance your own soul may be troubled and in need of guidance. It's only fair you get the chance to speak of your troubles. You're hereby summoned to speak in front of me on the morrow."

Sir Lambert blanched.

"My lord, I..."

"And bring your noble lady wife with you. I am certain she

would want to know of the ills which have plagued your soul," the bishop cut him off with a raised eyebrow.

There were guffaws from the crowd of onlookers, because it was plain from the bishop's words that he was well aware of Sir Lambert's transgressions and would address them soon. Tom wanted to shout with joy, yet he felt his heart clenching again in fear of what might happen to his woman, when the bishop beckoned him to come inside the Church, accompanied by Lord de Brunne. Tom turned to look at Beth, who was staring at him, wide-eyed and pale. She seemed determined to stride to where he was, but he cast her a look which held both warning and pleading. She held his eyes for a while, then at last nodded in mute resignation. Tom heaved a deep sigh of relief. Beth might be reckless but she was astute. It was plain she now understood her protests would not help in any way. The bishop would never listen to what she had to say.

Tom stepped inside the Church, relieved the elderly man's attention was now focussed upon him. Henry de Blois looked upon Tom in bored displeasure.

"I wouldn't have even deigned to look upon you if my nephew hadn't interceded. But now that I have, I feel it is my duty to know the circumstances of your sin. You live estranged from your wife?"

"I do, my lord."

"You're not to lie in church. What caused this estrangement?"

Tom knew that lying could not only seal his doom, but also Beth's, so he spoke the truth, although it was painful to speak it, "She lay with my brother, Your Grace."

The bishop crossed himself, then looked at Tom in sheer outrage.

"And you didn't denounce her?"

Tom shook his head.

"I did not, Your Grace."

"And where is she now? Not still cavorting with your brother?"

Tom couldn't now hide the truth, because he knew too well the bishop could unearth it if he wished it. He bowed his head mutely, loath to be speaking to a bishop of both his brother and of his wife, but knowing there was no return from it. He knew only too well where his brother was, and he would send word to him as soon as can be, so that Robin and Joanna could flee the Church's wrath.

"What is your brother's name and what's his craft?"

"He's Robin Reed, Your Grace. He is a builder," Tom had to answer.

"Robin Reed is your brother?" the bishop asked in sheer surprise. "A fine builder. I do like his work. In Durham foremost… Of late people have come to call this work of his the Galilee Chapel."

Tom nodded.

"And you agreed to this? That he and your wife live in sin? You condoned this?"

"Aye," Tom said, pushing his shoulders back.

The bishop shook his head in consternation. The young man in a monk's garb who accompanied the bishop suddenly bent to speak in his ear, and the bishop heaved a sigh.

"No wonder then. No wonder…"

Tom couldn't help but frown, because what the elderly man was saying didn't seem to make any sense.

Heaving a sigh, the bishop spoke, "Brother Timothy here knows of this from the Canon of Winchester and has just brought it to my attention. More than two months ago, Robin Reed lost his wife to childbirth. It's known to us, because he asked for permission to have her name inscribed within the stonework in the chapel he worked on, for remembrance. It is his wife everyone thought she was at the time, but now it seems plain to me that she wasn't. Joanna was her name, Brother Timothy recalls... Your own wife?"

Tom could do nothing but nod with a hard knot in his throat. "Aye, Joanna."

"God have mercy upon her soul, though she was plainly a sinner, and it is doubtless her sin caught up with her," the bishop said with a frown. "As for you, there's heavy penance you need to pay – both for allowing your own wife to live in sin, and also for luring a maiden into sin!"

Tom hung his head, not truly caring for his own fate. As long as Beth was spared, the rest did not matter. And now he couldn't help but think of Joanna, whom he'd once loved, now lying dead and cold in her grave.

"The penance you should serve..." the bishop started in a stern voice.

Yet he didn't have time to finish what he'd started though. Tristram de Brunne leant to speak to him very softly, and Tom saw the elderly man's eyebrows rise. He then began to confer with De Brunne in a low voice for a while, and then at last he cleared his throat:

"You'll spend this whole night on your knees in prayer, asking for God's mercy for your sins. And then..."

Again the elderly man cleared his throat.

"I saw the sword you made, hanging on my nephew's hip. Fine work. Fine work indeed. Finer than even Spanish swords, though you're not known mainly as a swordsmith. Our Lord loves hard work. So you shall work for His and the Church's Glory. Seven fine swords, with no charge for your hard toil, seems like fair penance to pay for your transgressions."

Tom nodded, too numb to feel any relief. However, he recalled himself enough to bow and kiss the bishop's ring, before the elderly man took his leave.

As soon as the bishop was gone, De Brunne patted Tom heartily on the back.

"All's well. He cares a lot for swords and baubles in this world. And now the old miser will be gone and he forgot all about the penance he thought it his duty to bestow upon your woman."

"Will Beth be safe?"

"Aye. She's off his mind, and Sir Lambert will be well and duly chastened. No one will dare go over a bishop's ruling. And the old man was so wrapped up in his love of swords, he well forgot to decree you marry your woman without delay, now that you're free." De Brunne then crossed himself and muttered, "But it is always sad news that another is dead. God have mercy on your poor wife's soul."

"May He be all-merciful," Tom said in his turn, far too overwhelmed to even make sense of what had occurred.

"Still," De Brunne added, "you should be thankful your penance is light compared to what I assume Uncle had in store. He has an unfortunate penchant for hair shirts. And once he even made me wear one. Be thankful he spared you that! Yet for this night you'll have to spend in prayer, I do not envy your knees," he finished with a slight wince.

Yet the night that Tom spent in Church with his head bent in prayer and upon his knees seemed more a blissful time to gather his thoughts, than a true punishment, in spite of the soreness and stiffness in his knees. He thought of Joanna and sincerely and fervently prayed her soul would find its peace. And he made his own final peace with her, no longer thinking upon what she'd done with bitterness. It no longer even appeared he'd brought himself to forgive her or his brother. To him it seemed now there was nothing to forgive. However briefly, Robin and Joanna had found love together, just as he and Beth had now done, and in his eyes such a love bond didn't truly need to be blessed in Church in order to be sacred. It was already sacred as it was. The bishop firmly believed it was Joanna's sin that had brought about her death. Yet Tom could not view what she'd done as a sin. He supposed this thought made him even more of a sinner than he really was, yet something inside himself, that strange side of his soul which could hear the rusty voice of iron call to him and understand its whisper, was plainly telling him it was not the greedy bishop but he himself who had the right of it. He knew though he would have to be careful not to share this thought, which would seem blasphemous, with anyone.

CHAPTER 14

It was with an unburdened soul and a light heart that Tom regained his home in the morning, even if his whole body was weary. Beth threw her arms around his neck, nearly smothering him with kisses, and seeming to care less about her fate than of his own.

"You took all the blame upon yourself! For me! What will you have to suffer now?" she asked in anguish.

He waved his hand, not wanting her to feel in any way in his debt for what it had been right of him to do.

"No suffering. Only toil."

Beth creased her brows into a frown when he told her of the bishop's penance upon him.

"They're all the same… Church men. Greedy and only seeking to satisfy their lusts."

"Aye. They're so. We should be grateful to Lord de Brunne though for this happy outcome. If it hadn't been for him, who knows what dire punishment the Church would have bestowed upon us."

She nodded.

"Still, I do not like the thought of you having to toil hard at their mercy."

He kissed the top of her head.

"I'll be, as always, at my Forge, and never at their mercy. And I'll have you by my side. Together we can make our own life."

She widened her eyes in sheer astonishment when he at last gave her the grim news of his wife's death.

"Sad news," she said, crossing herself. "Poor mother and poor child! I hope her soul will find its peace."

"And so do I," he told her gravely.

It was sad that his own fortune should spring from the suffering of those he'd held dear, but now he was free to marry the woman he loved. He wanted to marry Beth. While within himself he no longer set great store on Church blessings, he knew this needed to be done without delay in order to protect her.

"I am no longer wed," he told her pointedly. "I am now free to make a new life for myself."

"You wish for sons and daughters of your own, I know that already!" Beth said, glancing at him steadily.

He did. Always had. Yet he would not have them if this meant losing his love to childbirth.

"There is no rush. One day perchance. Or on no day at all. It is of no great matter to me," he said with a shrug, knowing he was, for the first time, breaking his promise to her of always being truthful.

"I have already spoken to the priest. We shall wed on the morrow," he added, understanding, by the way Beth was looking at him, that she knew only too well he craved children.

"On the morrow?"

"Aye," he nodded, hoping she saw it was the only course to take.

No one would ever call Beth a harlot again. She would be

safe from danger and from malice, and she would be able to walk with her head high among her peers from now on.

However, the next words Beth uttered simply astounded him.

"Nay," she muttered, with a forceful shake of her head.

He stared at her incredulously.

"You do not wish to wed me?"

"I… Not now. Not now… One day… You see, I…"

Beth looked simply flustered, but it was plain not only from her words, but from her eyes that she didn't in truth wish to marry him. She didn't wish to marry him even when she knew there was no other open course to them. She preferred danger and a brand of shame to being called his wife. Did she think so little of him then? Did she not love him at all? He'd thought he had her heart, just as she had his, but now it was plain she bore no true love for him.

He raked a hand through his hair, and then decided to rise to his weary feet. There was only one thing he could think of. So he headed for his Forge to work his fingers to the bone.

"Tom!" Beth called urgently after him, but he didn't heed her.

TOM HAD BECOME A COLD STRANGER, and he wouldn't speak to Beth, not even when she tried to plead with him. For two days now, he'd taken to sleeping on the floor of the kitchen, and always came to make his bed well after she was asleep in the bedchamber, leaving before dawn to work at his Forge. At first, she'd tried to talk to him, but she'd gotten rather angry herself at his cold contempt, and had given up attempting to make him see reason.

Could he not see how it hurt to be thought worthless in oneself? As long as she was not Tom's wife people thought her a harlot. As if her marriage to him would miraculously make her less sinful than she truly was and turn her from harlot to good woman. Beth supposed she had lost her faith in priests' and their words ever since Father Ambrose had attempted to force himself on her, then besmirched her good name when she'd not given in to his lechery. She'd not lost her faith in God though, and in what was right and true. And she already knew her love for Tom to be right and true.

Sharing his bed was not something she was ashamed of or that made her feel lesser. And she didn't want to get married to the man she loved just so the good people around her would no longer look upon her as if she was a harlot. Aye – she would certainly get married to Tom and bear his children, but in her own good time. And she wouldn't get married until all the people in the neighbourhood who thought her a woman without honour got to see her worth. She wanted them to have occasion to see her cleverness and her diligence. She wanted to walk with her head high not merely because she was Tom's wife, but because of her own accomplishments.

She sighed, understanding she was guilty of the sin of pride more than any other sin. And now, because of her pride, strife was threatening to break her apart from Tom. Wouldn't it be better to put her own foolish pride aside for once and agree to the sensible thing Tom had asked? Perchance she was indeed in the wrong for not wanting to marry him right away. Beth headed to the Forge, set on mending, at once, the rift with the man she loved.

Tom didn't seem to be busying himself with his craft when she sought him out. He was resting, and having his own lunch which, for two days now, he'd refused to share with her in the kitchen. Beth sat herself next to him.

"This has to end! We need to talk," she pressed, yet Tom was staring away from her as if she wasn't even there.

And his silence hurt her just as much as the contempt of those people who liked to call her a harlot. It was as if he, too, thought she meant nothing unless she wed him. Beth's willingness to mend their quarrel vanished into thin air, and she found herself stomping away from the Forge.

"Hateful man!" she muttered.

She supposed it was petty of her to behave as she did, when later, she began to berate the boys for making a pigsty of her clean kitchen.

"We have cleaned after ourselves," Declan shrugged impudently, although it was plain to Beth they had not.

She suddenly felt deeply sad and wearied and sat down, beginning to straighten her plait which had fallen in disarray.

"Fine. If you think you have, who am I to quarrel with you? It's plain you love living in a pigsty. It will be good then when I'm gone."

Three pairs of eyes at last came to attention.

"Gone?" Micah muttered rather mournfully.

Beth frowned, because she'd meant that the boys' laziness would be the death of her. She had no intention of going away from the place she'd already come to look upon as her home.

"Why won't you marry him?"

"Oh, it seems doors have ears!" Beth huffed. "It is my own business!"

"Ours too!" Declan countered. "You're making Master Tom unhappy. I've never seen him in a more foul temper, not even when Joanna lay with his brother, and, truth be told, I am loath to work with him at the Forge."

"*He* is unhappy? I tried to mend things between us and he treated me like I was nothing!"

"You hurt him!"

To Beth's surprise, it was William who spoke and he did with a set look on his face.

"I did not! All I meant was to wait a while before we get married!" Beth protested.

"You hurt him," William repeated in a quiet voice. "He now thinks you do not love him."

The other two looked at their friend in wonder and awe, then nodded to Beth.

"See, William already knows what's amiss. You hurt him," Declan repeated rather smugly.

Beth couldn't resist and smacked him over the head. It was a light smack, but Declan glared in sheer outrage.

"Are you daft?"

Beth didn't pay him any mind. She rolled her eyes, beginning to ask herself why this man of hers was unable to see she'd go through fire and brimstone for him, just as she already knew he'd face damnation for her.

"But why can't he see?" she muttered mostly to herself.

"That you're daft?" Declan ventured helpfully.

Yet as before, William seemed to already know how things stood.

"You will not marry him. Of course he thinks you do not love him."

"What? Why would he think I do not love him?"

"Daft woman! Any man in this world will think a woman doesn't love him if she won't marry him," Declan said in the same infuriating tone.

Beth frowned.

"Truly?" she muttered, because it seemed simply unfathomable to her why Tom hadn't already been able to see, no matter them being married or not, her heart would always be fully his.

William and Declan and Micah nodded eagerly.

"Now that you've botched things, you need to make them right," Micah cut in self-importantly.

"Aye," Declan joined in. "And nothing other than a good spanking can set things right again between the two of you."

"What?"

Declan should be thankful he was now within safe distance from her, because she would have given him another smack if she'd been able to.

"Think upon it," Micah supplied. "This thing between the two of you started with a spanking. It's only fitting that you mend things by yet another spanking."

Beth stormed away from the three boys who were obviously toying with her. Yet she began to think that their words, even if they'd been all a childish jest, might not be as amiss as she'd thought at first.

CHAPTER 15

"A beauty of a sword this will be!" Tristram de Brunne said wistfully. "Too bad you're fashioning it for my uncle…"

Tom nodded in some regret, yet hoped that one day Tristram's uncle would make a gift of the sword to a lord worthy of it.

"Some ale, my lord?" Beth's voice cut the flow of his thoughts.

He frowned even upon hearing her voice, because she had, after all, broken his heart. His back was turned on her, and he wouldn't look at her, but he saw De Brunne's eyes simply widen. He hastily turned to see what was amiss. Upon a usual day, Beth wore her hair in a single plait down her back, but now she wore it loose and she'd bedecked it with flowers. She was clad in her Sunday gown, and was swishing her well rounded hips like a temptress as she was walking to them, tray in hand. Tom supposed he had to be thankful she'd not yet had time to finish her new gown. He felt certain that, had the new gown been ready, she would have worn it now in order to make herself look even more bewitching than she already was.

He cast his woman a dark glare. If she thought he'd forgive her so soon for breaking his heart just because she looked bewitching, then she was sadly mistaken. Yet, Beth didn't even spare him a glance as she approached, tray in hand.

"Ale, my lord?" she said, extending a cup to De Brunne, who nodded silently.

"How does it taste?" Beth suddenly asked in a sultry voice, and De Brunne seemed nearly to choke upon his ale hearing her words.

Tom told himself this was all a bad dream. This was not Beth. Why was she flaunting herself in front of De Brunne like that? The lord looked flustered, not knowing how to act in front of a woman who was so blatantly trying to catch his eye. And, while soon Tom began to understand only too well why Beth was behaving this way, it didn't change things at all. Tom resolved at once she was flaunting herself in order to stir his anger and to get him to talk to her.

It was fortunate De Brunne was an honourable man, and he made a hurried departure as soon as was possible, choosing to run away from Beth's blatant regard rather than behave improperly to another man's woman. This left Beth staring after the lord with a sigh, and toying with her hair as if she was indeed the giggling simpleton she now pretended to be. Tom tried to stare away from her, but couldn't, and found himself casting her a dark glare.

"What is amiss?" Beth asked, giving him a guileless smile.

Tom prepared to retreat, yet he found her blocking his path.

"Something amiss then?" she asked again with an arched eyebrow.

Tom felt he could no longer control his temper, and found himself hoisting her over his shoulder. He was so enraged that he only belatedly realized he was heading for their chamber. *It couldn't be helped now, could it?* he thought in sheer fury, as he closed the door behind him and threw his woman unceremoniously on the bed.

He stopped himself in time from crudely parting her legs and pushing inside her roughly right then and there. The picture in his mind was enticing, and he imagined himself slamming in and out of her with a vengeance, yet he made himself step away from the bed.

"Oh," Beth said and it seemed her voice was filled with as much disappointment as he himself was feeling at this time.

"You're angry with me," she added in a blatantly regretful voice, which made him want to strangle her.

"And you are right to be angry with me," she added. "I have behaved wretchedly!"

"You think?" he snarled.

"I know I fully deserve a punishment for the way I acted," Beth said, and her voice sounded as infuriatingly contrite as before.

He stared at her, clenching his fists and knowing his temper was hanging upon a very thin thread.

"But, see, I've even cut a switch for you to use in order to amend my behaviour. It's plain I'm in need of a stern lesson," she cooed, with a serene smile upon her face.

Now she was plainly mocking him. And at this point, Tom decided he'd had enough.

"A switch?" he asked, as his eyes fell upon the implement she'd named, which was already lying on a pillow in their bed.

Beth beamed.

"Will it do, you think?"

Tom cursed both her and himself under his breath. So this was the game she wished to play? Fine. Then the game was on. Though he doubted that at the end of it *he* would be the one crying his eyes out. He went to the bed, making a show of testing the switch against his palm.

"'Twil serve," he said tersely.

He didn't give her time to say anything more. He placed the pillow in the middle of the bed, and he made her lie over it on her belly, making short work of hoisting her skirts. The pillow served its purpose, because Beth's bare bottom was now thrust towards him, in a position for him to put the switch to good use. He didn't waste any more time.

"Ouch!"

Beth's voice was filled with surprise at the sting of this new implement, whose touch she probably found somewhat unexpected. Tom suppressed a half-satisfied half-malicious grin, because, having been on the receiving end of this implement several times in his childhood, he knew only too well how much it stung. Yet, while its sting during the punishment was fierce, the damage from it was mild in the end, even milder in fact than that which his big blacksmith's hand could bestow upon Beth's behind. So Tom went on with his switching, beginning to paint pink and then red stripes upon the bottom of the woman who'd taunted him to spank her. It had been her wish to receive a stern lesson, hadn't it? So that was what he was in truth providing. The very lesson she'd asked for.

He hadn't been counting, yet it was perhaps on the fifth lash of his switch that Beth began to sniff, and asked in a quivering voice, "Tom, don't you think I've already learnt my lesson?"

He smiled to himself wickedly.

"I think not," he replied, brandishing the switch with even more vigour.

Beth bucked and wriggled under the new, harder lashes she received, yet, to her credit, she didn't attempt to leave her position or protect her bottom in any way.

"Ah... It stings so!" she complained at last, in a voice that already seemed to be filling with tears.

"And so it should!" Tom countered, hardening his heart against her.

Yet, he laid the switch only a couple of more times upon her rounded bottom, shaking his head to himself, and knowing his anger against her was already beginning to melt. Foolish, stubborn woman! What had she thought to accomplish by goading him so? Did she think by angering him further he'd forgive her for not loving him at all? For not wanting to be bound to him?

Beth was already crying softly, when he discarded the switch, flinging it aside.

"You asked for this," he found himself muttering grimly, seating himself on the bed and beginning to rub his temples.

She attempted to sit up, but at this time his spanking must still sting fiercely, so she chose to remain lying on her belly.

"It is not at all as you seem to think. It is not because I don't love you, you know," she told him quite suddenly in a tearful voice.

There was something simply heart breaking in her voice, and, at this moment, while she hadn't uttered downright that she loved him, Tom understood she was in truth telling him she really did. He'd gotten to know Beth in the months they'd spent together. And she was not a woman who would ever utter the words 'I love thee' outright. That she'd brought herself to even say as much as she had to him was something he should cherish. He still didn't understand why she wouldn't bind herself to him in Church, but at this moment, it no longer mattered.

"*Dearling,*" he said, now cross with himself for having judged her unfairly in thinking she didn't care for him.

It was plain she did. And he'd been foolish enough to let himself get carried away by anger and mistrust.

"Forgive me!" he said, moving to bestow an ardent kiss on her lips.

Her face was tear-stained and her nose blotchy, but to Tom it seemed she'd never looked more beautiful.

"You really set my bottom on fire, you know!" she complained, with a small sniff which hid a half smile.

Tom shrugged with a sheepish grin.

"I wasn't asking your forgiveness for that."

She creased her brow.

"You weren't?"

"I wasn't. I was asking you to forgive me for the way I acted towards you in the past days. Yet," he added pointedly, wagging his finger, "that didn't mean you should have behaved like that to De Brunne!"

When she tarried to answer, he patted her spanked bottom lightly, which was now rather deliciously striped with red.

~

Beth stirred under Tom's touch, seized by both tantalizing pain and scorching pleasure. What he did at the next moment was something he'd not done before. Bending his head, he began to lick the very stripes he'd mercilessly bestowed upon her earlier. His tongue was soothing and stirring at the same time, like a balm on her poor scorched bottom, yet, at the same time…

"I can see how much you're enjoying this, Tom Reed! My misery and discomfort after your hard spanking!" She made a show of complaining.

Tom chuckled softly.

"I suppose that as a blacksmith I've got used to trying to bend metal to my will."

"Is that what you mean to achieve by spanking me? Bend me to your will?" she asked with an arched eyebrow, not liking the thought.

"Yet as a blacksmith," he added as he began to brush his fingers across the red stripes on her behind, "I am always aware that metal always has a will of its own."

"Still, you keep trying to bend it."

"Aye, but metal is far more stubborn than you think and it always has a very good memory. It always recalls the first shape it was first wielded in. And the blacksmith may think he has managed to mould it to his liking, but he never does in truth mould it. As years pass, it is perchance the metal that in truth moulds him."

Beth laughed with a shake of her head.

"You're not as unskilful with words as you sometimes lead others to think. Now you've started to speak like a minstrel. But I cannot fathom what you're trying to tell me."

"What I was trying to say is that it is not only you who bends to my will, but I also bend to yours, even when I take it upon myself to teach you a lesson."

She heaved a sigh.

"Is that meant to make me feel better about the sore bottom you've given me?"

Yet she could well see what Tom was trying to tell her. She didn't feel he lorded over her, not even when he spanked her, and, in truth, Tom was never unfair or overbearing. As for the spankings... She had to admit it to herself she'd already ceased to view them as discipline. They were all in truth love play, although she already knew that neither she nor Tom would ever openly call them that. It was the way things stood between them, and it was far more diverting not to call them by their true name. Because it was like that between Tom and her – some things were better not spoken in words. They were beyond words, just as her love for him.

"You know too well I love you. Marry me!" he urged her, and kissed her ardently.

She'd been unfair to him, and she was well aware of it. And it would be the right, sensible thing to say aye to what he was asking. Yet she still had a stubbornness of her own, and he needed to see it was not for the pleasure of refusing him that she was doing this.

"I will. One day," she said soothingly.

He frowned upon her.

"Not now?"

"One day," she vowed looking steadily into his eyes.

She didn't want to speak the words to him that would make him understand. She just wanted him to see this for himself and simply trust her judgement. For a moment it seemed he was again angry with her. But, after he stared at her for a while, he shook his head, raking his dark hair in that way of his that had become so dear to her.

"Fine, stubborn woman. As you wish. As long as that day doesn't come when I'm old and on my deathbed."

"It won't!" she vowed, brushing a light kiss upon his taut lips.

EPILOGUE

It was little more than a year later that Beth came upon Tom saying she had to speak to him of a certain matter. He had been, as usual, engrossed in his work at the Forge, but he was alone at this time.

"Something amiss?" he asked, putting his hammer down, because it was unlike Beth to come upon him in the middle of his work.

She was usually just as busy as he was, with sundry chores of her own, which now involved not only their trade and household, but many other errands and visits she made around the city. She was different from him, and always ready to laugh and talk and gossip with those she came to call her friends. And Tom had begun to see she'd made a lot of friends, many among the wives of the craftsmen and tradesmen in the neighbourhood. By now, there was no one left in their neighbourhood who seemed to think ill of Beth, as they'd gotten to know her and see her worth. For some months already, everyone had been calling her Mistress Reed, and they spoke of her as if she'd long been Tom's wife. Tom himself had gotten so used to this that at times he truly forgot Beth and he were not married in Church true and proper, even if the priest chided them every month for tarrying. In truth, busy with his work as he was, lately he'd not even recalled to renew the one question that, for a while, he'd asked her every single day.

"How fare you, *dearling*?" he inquired now, coming to softly brush his hand against her cheek, because he suddenly perceived she looked rather pale and tired.

He chastised himself for not paying more mind to his woman, and silently vowed to watch her more closely from now on. He loved to work hard, and didn't tire easily. But that didn't mean that those around him couldn't tire when far too much was put upon their shoulders.

Beth shrugged away his question with a smile.

"You do recall the vow I made you?" she asked him rather suddenly.

"Which of them?" Tom countered in a soft voice, now tracing the sweet curve of her cheek.

In truth, she'd made several vows to him, among which that of behaving herself. But that was a vow she never seemed to keep.

"You know... The one I promised I'd fulfil long before you're old and on your deathbed," Beth told him pointedly.

His heart skipped a beat, because he'd become nearly resigned she'd never want to marry him in Church.

"Ha...the vow," he muttered as if he couldn't quite recall it, because he was unable to resist having his own revenge on Beth for rejecting him the first time he'd asked.

She punched his arm.

"Oh, *that* vow," he added with a mischievous grin.

He simply couldn't help himself. He added even more mischief.

"What makes you certain I still want to marry you?"

She glared at him, and he shrugged, then went on, because it was far too tempting not to.

"Or perchance I should answer just as you did. *One day.* Yet, to be sure, before you're old and on your deathbed."

Another punch landed on his arm, and this was one he felt somewhat.

"Not one day, Tom Reed. As soon as can be, because I'll have no wagging tongues about the child we're bound to have," Beth scolded.

For a moment, the Forge seemed to be spinning around him. The first thought which came upon him then was that he should feel joy. But then his heart was seized with fear. He felt afraid of what might happen to both Beth and their unborn child.

"Tom, look at me," his woman told him in a soothing voice. "You've naught to fear. I know all will be well."

If someone else had uttered the words, Tom would not have brought himself to believe them, but he had come to set great faith in this woman of his. So he chose to believe Beth, thinking she must already have the right of it. All would be well.

R. R. VANE

I discovered romance in a shop which sold used books when I was a teen and I have been writing romance novels in my head ever since. My first ever draft was a medieval romance with a gray-eyed knight, and I still want to finish it one day. For me writing is a dream come true and I always try to stay true to my dreams. So I write historical/paranormal/fantasy romance. My first book (*A Deep Dark Call,* published as Rose Vane) is a Gothic romance set in nineteenth-century Romania. *A Stern Knight for My Lady* is the first medieval romance I ever published.

Visit her website here:
https://rosevane.com/

Don't miss these exciting titles by R. R. Vane and Blushing Books!

Her Stern Husband Series
A Stern Lord for My Lady
The Blacksmith's Woman

BLUSHING BOOKS

Blushing Books is the oldest eBook publisher on the web. We've been running websites that publish steamy romance and erotica since 1999, and we have been selling eBooks since 2003. We have free and promotional offerings that change weekly, so please do visit us at http://www.blushingbooks.com/free.

BLUSHING BOOKS NEWSLETTER

Please join the Blushing Books newsletter
to receive updates & special promotional offers.
You can also join by using your mobile phone:
Just text BLUSHING to 22828.

Every month, one new sign up via text messaging will receive a $25.00 Amazon gift card, so sign up today!

www.ingramcontent.com/pod-product-compliance
Lightning Source LLC
LaVergne TN
LVHW090950080826
845145LV00003B/959

* 9 7 8 1 6 3 9 5 4 0 1 9 8 *